Dial 999

A Jon Hunter Mystery

By H. L. Raven

Reality Asylum Books

This is a work of historical fiction, which takes place from April 30 to May 19, 1977. Any references to historical events, real people, or real locales are used fictitiously. Other names, characters, places, and incidents are the product of the author's imagination, and any resemblance to actual events or locales or persons, living or dead, is entirely coincidental.

Cover art by Elisabeth Butler

Library of Congress Control Number: 2010910693
ISBN-10 0-9718673-1-3
ISBN-13 978-0-9718673-1-4

Reality Asylum Books
(An Imprint of Via Dolorosa Press)
701 East Schaaf Road
Cleveland, OH 44131-1227   USA

I wish to thank the following people in particular, without whom this book would not exist:

My parents, Gary & Debbie Steely, who still loved and supported me even when I made them listen to Crass, Sex Gang Children, and The Cure's *Pornography* album over and over again; my brother, Matthew Steely, who bore the brunt of my eccentricity; my husband, Richard Burns, for waiting on me hand-and-foot while I was a writing diva; Sarah Glazer, a constant inspiration as well as one of the greatest writers I've ever known; Kimber Smith for her encouragement and kitty-watching; and Mick Mercer, whose experience and friendship all these years are appreciated beyond words.

For

Mara Morrigan

a ghrá mo chroí

London's burning
with boredom now...
London's burning
dial 99999

ONE

When Miranda slumped over onto the floor, I knew it was time to go.

She had been sitting on the chipped tile in the bathroom, using the toilet as a prop for her arm and mumbling incessantly to my shadow as I inspected my bleeding nose. I could see her reflection in the mirror, wiping at the side of her face with her dirty fingers after she sniffled a couple times.

"You've got to hit the vein just right," she said to me, slapping the crease of her inner arm. "And if you don't know the difference between a vein and an artery, you're fucked."

Strands of tousled brown hair clung to her reddened cheeks from perspiration, and her eyes narrowed in concentration on the task at hand.

I stuffed a thin wad of toilet paper up my nose, hoping to absorb some of the blood. "I don't know why you waste your time with that shit, Miranda." My teeth clenched for a minute.

Miranda smirked, having found a good vein.

"You could use a right jab yourself, Jon. I mean, it's a party, innit?"

≠

We were at Bugs' and Tony's flat in Clerkenwell, our usual hangout, recuperating from a Teddy Boy run-in. The original plan for the evening was to catch a Buzzcocks show at The Roxy, but the 'cancelled' sign on the doors meant that wasn't going to happen. Instead, we got caught up in the now-traditional Saturday Teds-vs-punks brawl. Boise Lou and his gang were set on roughing us up good, but we only lasted about a half an hour before we got bored and retreated back to our mates' gaff.

Their flat was part of an old warehouse that they converted into living space. The focal point was the large entry room littered with sofas, card tables, and folding chairs—perfect for drinks and poker games. With such an open area, it was just the right place for parties. We all took advantage of that at any opportunity, much to our mates' delight as they loved being hosts to chaos. The neighborhood back then was rough, but Bugs and Tony had a safe haven, helped, certainly, by the group of thugs that lived two floors above. *"They're family,"* Tony would remind me after a few drinks, *"and my family looks out for you, Jonny boy."*

Despite his hard exterior, though, Tony was a decent guy. I think his attitude came out of the fact that he was shorter than all the other blokes. Kind of a puffing up of the feathers to show everyone he was on the same level. He had some bollocks, Tony did. He dressed like an early Teddy Boy (in '40's style suits), which actually fit him quite well, but he did it just to be a wanker. The Teds knew he was one of us, not one of them, which only served to wind them up. Bugs thrived on those displays of aggression. The crazy energy that made him so much fun to be around was also the same thing that made you want to keep him within your sight. He was a ticking time-bomb waiting for the right moment to explode. Everything about him was wrong: his hair, a shock of blonde burned white and brittle with peroxide; his face, scratched and pocked from dancing, fighting, or acne—I couldn't tell which; his clothes, ripped and torn and salvaged.

It didn't take long for us to raid the flat once we burst through the doors. We adjusted furniture, cleaned out the liquor cabinet, and increased the noise level within minutes. The sound of our voices, Tony's record player, and police sirens scouring the streets was like static against the metallic interior of the room. Thick dust shrouded the cracked window panes, hiding the glare of the street lamps. Many of the high-hanging light fixtures in the room were either broken or burned-out. To compensate, Bugs wired the perimeter of the room in twisted strings of Christmas (or *fairy*, as the Brits corrected me) lights. Garlands of little bulbs, both clear and multi-colored, sparkled against the tinfoil that papered the walls. Some blinked in measured time, others flickered only when you bumped them.

Tony was near the kitchen chatting up Susan, trying to use his infamous skills in persuasion to get a shag. He had been buying her drinks earlier in the evening as a warm-up exercise, and now he was laying the charm on heavy. I could tell by the way his beady brown eyes softened that the magic must be working.

Susan smiled at me as Tony began talking with his hands. She looked out-of-place in her clean, department-store outfit, but she was one of us just the same. My girl Mary met her through a mutual friend and shared a flat with her near King's Cross station. Despite the fact that she wasn't a punk, Susan seemed to take to most of us. She was actually a pleasant change of pace in our circle of friends, so when Mary invited her to join us, it didn't matter that she wasn't fond of the Sex Pistols; we liked her anyway.

Dancing near the record player were a couple blokes I recognized as Roxy regulars with Susan's friend Julie in between them. Julie was wriggling around, her blonde hair grazing her cheeks as she moved. She was definitely the popular girl in our group—due in large part to her carefree nature and the fact that she looked like Debbie Harry. Lately I had noticed Bugs taking an interest in her, and I assumed that flirting with these random guys was her way of telling Bugs to move things along a bit faster.

Mary, in the meantime, was cheering from the poker table. Her Irish accent was telltale in a room full of Cockney blokes, and no matter how many different colors she'd try dyeing her hair, her fair features, sprinkling of freckles, and bright green eyes gave away her true heritage. She was a feisty little thing, which was something that attracted me to her in the first place, but which also got her into trouble. As now, laughing a bit to myself, I could see Bugs drunkenly lecturing her on what it meant to keep a 'poker face'.

"Okay, mate, what about this one then?" Paul asked, snapping my attention back to him. We had been comparing bruises between pints, a friendly sort of competition Paul and I started the previous year when I moved to London from the

States. Paul had successfully encouraged a long scar on his dark arm from the cut he got at a Johnny Thunders show back in February, and he displayed it proudly. All I could find on myself were a handful of fresh scratches and the feeling of something on my face that might be purple in the morning. Nothing major, especially compared to this bloke Paul knew back in Kingston who would brand himself when he was bored.

Just as Paul started describing to me the branding process, Bugs yelled out *"Gangrene!"* and we all snapped our heads to look.

Shit, I thought.

Gangrene was Dan Green, a junkie who tended to be nothing but trouble. We called him Gangrene because he rarely went to the hospital for treatment after fights, which left his body a constant black-and-blue mess. He was a scruffy sort of guy, choosing to be a squatter and making his living peddling highly-addictive substances. We all thought he was a right nasty piece of work, and if questioned we wouldn't admit to knowing him. But, after all was said and done, he still somehow ended up a mate. (Though an uninvited one at that!)

Gangrene stumbled into the flat, tripping over Tony's feet and knocking Susan's drink onto her clothes. Tony shoved Gangrene's bruised shoulder, drunk and angry.

"Oi! Piss off!" Tony spat, following with a collection of colorful Cockney obscenities.

I cringed slightly, expecting Gangrene to punch back, but he just stumbled further into the room, grabbing hold of Bugs' shirt sleeve to steady himself. Bugs laughed at Gangrene, spilling his lager on the floor. Gangrene's feet slipped a bit in the drink, but Bugs was anchored, and they merely wobbled in their drunkenness.

When I got up for another pint a while later, I saw Nigel come out of the bathroom, half-clothed. His tight black jeans were unbuttoned at the fly, and he wandered out shirtless, wiping his sweaty forehead with the back of his hand. He motioned to me for a cigarette.

"She was a good lay, mate," Nige said when he reached me, smoothing out his shaggy brown hair. He was referring to Miranda, the girl he brought back from outside The Roxy.

"Told her she could leave now?" I teased. Nige wasn't exactly known for relationships that lasted longer than the time it took to fuck.

Nige chuckled. "Yeah, but she's in with Gangrene."

We both shrugged. *Heroin.* Nige and I kept away from that shit.

"Junkie tart," Nige snickered, taking a drag from the cigarette.
He headed towards Bugs and Mary who were falling off their chairs laughing about something. Bugs was reaching for Mary's arm,

but he only connected with the stretchy material of her top. She tumbled onto the floor, giggling. Although she was nearly 18, she had the soft, sweet face of a teen much younger, and that made the scene more perverse than it was. Bugs laid back on the floor, face-up, trying to catch his breath. Mary slowly pulled herself back onto the chair, but by that time the poker game had ended. She glanced over at me, blowing a kiss as she steadied herself against the table.

I just wasn't feeling like myself tonight. My limbs were heavy, as if I had gained weight, but I was still the same thin bloke. Wiry, even. Was I tired? Bored? Everyone around me was having a grand time; what was my problem?

By this time, Julie had joined Bugs on the floor and they were snogging. Someone broke the needle on the record player and Nige was trying to replace it before the flat was destroyed in protest.

As I returned to Paul, Gangrene bumped into me. He could barely stand up, his eyes were struggling to stay open, and he reeked of alcohol and sweat.

"Jon, mate," he greeted in a complete stupor. He patted me on the back drunkenly and before I could tell him to bugger off, he hobbled off to the door.

Paul shook his head watching Gangrene leave.

"Bloody nose," he said as he turned back to me.

"Yeah, guess so," I replied, chuckling. That was a new one to me. These British with their silly insults.

"No, mate, bloody nose!" Paul pointed at my face.

I felt my nose with my fingertips. He was right. A Teddy Boy cracked his fist into my face during our earlier tussle, but I could have sworn the bleeding had stopped before we reached Clerkenwell.

In the bathroom, Miranda leaned towards my leg, her eyes fogging. She offered me a shot with an unsteady hand. Her cheeks were flushed and her lip quivered–the shit must have been good. I declined and watched the syringe drop into her lap. "Your loss, Jon," she said softly, trailing off. "Your loss..." Her eyelids closed and she smiled once before hitting her head on the floor.

I nudged her with my boot. She let out a final moan before slipping into her dreamy state.

"You're pathetic, you know that?" I said to her. "It's about time someone told you the truth."

It was so easy to have a captive audience when your audience was blacked-out, drooling on the floor. So I continued with my memorized tirade, having saved this one for such an occasion:

"You call yourself a punk, but for what? You're not changing the system; you're lying in a fucking dirty toilet being just what the government wants you to be. Just a fucking slave."

I shoved my boot into her again, only this time I wasn't so careful about it. She didn't make a noise so I stood there wanting to yell at her about something else. But then it seemed irrelevant. Tony was right–when you tell people things they don't want to hear, they start acting like you don't even exist.

So this is what it comes down to, that little nagging voice in my head said to me. There I was, right in the middle of London and bored out of my bloody mind. I had feverishly agreed to move to my aunt's house in England with the hope that I would be able to be a part of the growing punk scene. A scene I thought held more meaning in the UK than the one that had been spawn in America. But I was discovering that it wasn't as idyllic as I dreamed; challenging the world was giving way to strung-out complacency. Hell, I could have stayed back home in Cleveland listening to The Dead Boys if I just wanted to call myself 'punk'. I wanted to be part of a movement, a force of change. The American scene was choked with drugs already, and I thought, naively perhaps, that it would be different here in England. And it was, for a while. But now... I just felt so useless, in the same rut I was back in the States. Something had to happen; something just had to give.

I was still staring at Miranda and getting more disgusted as the moments passed. I wanted to shake her back to reality. Was I on a crusade? Maybe. Anarchy was one thing, but this? What the fuck was she doing?

And Gangrene didn't help matters any. He supplied Miranda and countless others as the big dealer. It used to just be sulfate, an amphetamine, but now Gangrene seemed to have his hands full with heroin. And everywhere you saw his bruised body, you knew there followed in his wake junkies looking for a fix. People were willing to pay good money for whatever Gangrene had, and it was no secret that he had better drugs than anyone. Gangrene and I had fought over this repeatedly. Fist fights, even. But it came down to him making a living and me making yet another stand. I was clapped out. And so I gave up on him. I folded.

Now here I stood, a junkie at my feet and a wad of tissue stiff with blood in my hand. My nose felt dry, but I stared in the mirror for another few minutes to be sure.

Out in the main room of the flat, Tony was beyond drunk and Bugs had started another poker game. Mary was finishing a pint.

"What's wrong, luv?" she asked, setting the empty bottle aside. "You've been so quiet all night."

I shrugged.

Mary's lips curled into a sly sort of smile. "I've got an idea..."

My eyebrow raised in interest. Mary was a treasure trove of craziness—some of her ideas were insane, some were illegal, but all ended up being fun. Perhaps this would be just what I needed to pull myself out of this funk.

"Come on," she said, leading me to the door.

Behind us, Susan called out something to Tony from the bathroom.

Tony was laughing and holding onto Bugs in an attempt to stand up, his lager spilling over the poker table. "Suz... Suz...," he gasped, trying to speak between choking laughter, "just drag her into the hall... and let her sleep it off."

≠

I lived in a council block on Hardwick Street, north of Clerkenwell in Finsbury. It was a bit of a walk from Bugs' and Tony's flat, and not quite a pleasant one, so I traveled briskly in the dark with Mary gathered close.

My flat was on the top floor of a building whose amenities varied daily. Some days we had warm water, other days we traded that for consistent electricity. In the winter we might be surprised with heat every third day, in the summer we might rejoice for the four hours our refrigerators worked. But the rent was cheap, and that's all that mattered to me. This particular evening the lift was unavailable, so we exercised our way up the stairs.

By the time we reached my flat, we were doubled-over, panting. The door was stuck again, and it took the weight of both of us to push through. Mary fell face-first onto the floor, and I tripped over her shoe, sending myself crashing down alongside her. We coughed as we laughed, the air in the room hot and humid from the radiator.

"All right, luv," Mary said, her voice fading softly away from me in the darkness, "about my idea..."

I sat up, pulling off my boots and tossing my jacket aside. There were a couple clicks of the lamp in the corner, but no light. No power tonight, apparently.

"Léan air!" Mary grumbled in Irish.

Then I heard the clinking of jewelry against glass and a dull thud as an empty pint bottle fell to
the carpet. I crawled toward the noise, taking down a kneeling Mary. She struggled a bit, gasping as I nipped at any skin within mouth's reach.

"I've got matches in my pocket," I mumbled between mouthfuls of soft flesh.

Mary said nothing, just let out a low moan of approval. Her small hands felt around at my waist. To help matters, I leaned forward a little, holding her close to me as I traced circles into the taught skin of her neck with my tongue. Mary's hands slipped into my front pockets, and she searched thoroughly for the matches, minutes even, before giving up to search behind. Half a pack of matches was in my back pocket, and there Mary's fingers went, removing the flattened box (though not before giving my bum a little squeeze).

She handed me the box, and I tried showing off by lighting a match with my front teeth. It didn't quite work that way, and while I was gagging on the residue, Mary struck one and held it up, looking around quickly for something to ignite so that we could see. An old newspaper was on the floor, so she crumpled up a page over my ashtray, flicked the flame into it, and watched the pile light up. I climbed off of her and hurriedly unearthed some candle nubs which we fitted into empty pint bottles as make-shift lamps.

"Now then, what's this new plot, Maire?"

I pulled out two bottles of still-cool beer from the refrigerator and handed her one.

Mary was being swallowed into the old couch, her feet dangling over the edge. "You Americans and your cold ale!" she grimaced.

I chuckled and raised my bottle to her in a casual toast.

She smiled wide, like she had an uncontainable secret. Her red lipstick was smeared on her thin lips, giving off the look of a deranged starlet.

"Well, I was chatting with Caoilinn yesterday and we thought maybe we could start our own fanzine."

Her kohl eyes were eager, and she continued quickly before I got the chance to dismiss the idea. "I mean, Mark's got one, Shane's got one... And I know a bloke who can run off copies for us. Want to? Please?"

If Caoilinn (or Keely, as I called her) suggested it, there was no stopping Mary. She and Mary had been lovers and were still so, despite the fact that Keely stayed behind in Ireland. That didn't bother me—the rule among us punks was that nobody was really anybody's.

In fact, Keely and I got along quite well. And we had more than just Mary in common—a love of political debate and philosophical literature, a desire to be in the center of a revolution, a need to create a destiny for our own selves... *"Why don't you just shag her already then, if you love her so much,"* Bugs chided me once. But that's not how it was with us. She had Mary and I had Mary and Mary had both of us and that's how it worked. Nothing more, nothing less.

Keely was incredibly creative, so it was no surprise to me that she might have come up with this idea. I took a swig of my beer and considered. There were a few guys I knew back in the States who had their own fanzines—quirky, do-it-yourself publications. Scrubs in Cincinnati printed a zine called *Spazilytic Converter* where he basically discussed all the ways you could make piercings and jewelry from old car parts. And a buddy of mine back in home in Cleveland ran *Still Dead*, a Dead Boys fanzine. He even gave out badges to the person who could send in the most "Spot Stiv Bators" photos. Mary could be on to something here. Something fun.

"Yeah, I'm up for it."

Mary clapped excitedly, fully chuffed.

"Do you think Mr. White will let us set out copies?" she asked. Mr. White owned the tiny record shop where Paul and I worked.

"I don't see why not. When should we start?"

Mary insisted that it be as soon as possible. I insisted that she head to my bedroom and fast. All this talk of having fun led my mind to other avenues.

I blew out the candles while Mary pulled herself out of the couch. Then, on all-fours, I crawled after her, tugging various pieces of her clothing off before we reached my bed. She draped herself across my crumpled sheets. Her white skin absorbed the moonlight that refracted and filtered through my broken window, making her glow a bit against the shadows in the room. I couldn't seem to get rid of my clothes quickly enough. Mary extended one of her legs to rub against me, curling her toes into my thigh like a kneading kitten. My pulse thumped so loudly that I almost couldn't hear her urging me on. I felt starved, and I preyed upon her savagely. My neighbor in the next flat pounded on the wall, so I knew I was doing something right.

The blaring ring-ring of the phone startled me out of my sleep in the morning. At first it didn't register with me, and I knocked my alarm clock onto the floor. When I realized what the noise was, I felt around to see if Mary was awake. Aside from myself and a pile of linens that now needed washing, the bed was empty. It must have been at least the tenth set of rings before I picked up the receiver.

It was Bugs.
And he was screaming.

TWO

Miranda was dead.

Bugs found her the next morning curled up behind the sofa. The police were asking what happened, but Bugs had no clue. And judging by his phone call, he was getting desperate. When it came down to it, I might have been the last person to talk to her. And if that was the case, the cops wanted to know what I knew.

When I got to the flat, Miranda was being carried out on a stretcher. I sideswiped a younger policeman chewing on his pen as I squeezed through the door. Tony was sobering up the hard way, answering police questions in spurts. His responses reflected the fact that he wasn't all that conscious last night to remember much of anything.

"*Jon! Jon, mate!*" Bugs wheezed. His gaunt face was strained and drained of color. He reached out for my arm and pulled me over. The police looked at me as their next victim.

One of the constables pulled out a small notepad. "Name and address, please."

I took a final drag on my cigarette and flicked it to the floor, putting it out with my boot. "Jon Hunter, Farringdon Towers, Hardwick Street, Finsbury."

The cop looked up before writing. "American, eh?"

I cleared my throat and nodded once. My accent.

"Can I see your registration papers?"
Fuck.

I felt around in my trouser pockets, but he caught on. He waved over a tall, stately-looking officer who was dressed differently than the others, almost as though he were off-duty.

"Edwards, I think you better check this one out," the cop said to him.

The constable from the doorway appeared when Edwards approached and stood like a gun to my back, adding: "Just routine, son." His Cockney accent seemed almost sarcastic.

Edwards took the officer's notebook, carefully reviewing the comments made.

"So, what happened here last night, Mr. Hunter?" he asked. His voice was serious, but not abrasive. He looked at me almost gently, yet something about his eyes reminded me not to get too comfortable.

My story to him was terse; I learned from little adventures back home that you tell a cop only as much as you have to and nothing more.

The constable behind me crouched down to the floor, looking around for something. "You say it was heroin, then?"

I nodded. Bugs was still standing beside me, but now looked as though he would be sick.

"Try the toilet, Jeffreys," Edwards said to the officer searching at my feet.

Jeffreys got up and made his way towards the hall, all the while checking the floor.

Edwards scribbled one more thing in the notebook and then slipped it into his jacket. His face softened momentarily.

"You young people need to be a bit more serious about your lives."

Bugs reached a hand up and rubbed the side of his head. His cropped hair was mashed and stuck down on one side, as if he had fallen asleep in a puddle of lager.

I bit my tongue in anticipation of any response Bugs could give to the lecture it sounded like Edwards had for us. If Edwards knew what was good for him, he'd leave it at that. But he continued:

"I see this all too often now, especially with you *punks*."

Bugs straightened up next to me, his eyes narrowing. "And what the bloody hell's that supposed to mean, then?" he shot back.

Edwards looked directly at him and responded calmly: "I mean that you punks always seem to be looking for trouble. Drugs, violence— what does it get you in the end?"

Bugs' fists clenched, and he moved forward a bit. I grabbed his arm, gritting my teeth. *Fucking stop, man*, I thought to myself. *Don't prove the pig right!*

Jeffreys returned with Miranda's syringe in a little plastic bag.

"Well then," Edwards said, acknowledging Jeffreys. "I think we're done here."

Jeffreys nodded. "You should watch the kind of people you're mates with. It could land you in real trouble some day." He sneered at us like a right bastard.

The shock from finding Miranda was wearing off Bugs. He lunged forward, shoving Jeffreys (who was back to chewing on his pen) into Edwards.

"So, you think being a fucking cunt like you is better, then?" Bugs rammed the heels of his hands against Jeffreys again. "A fucking pig, then?"

I tried pulling him back, but he kicked my shin.

Jeffreys threw his pen down and punched Bugs in the jaw. Edwards just stepped aside, frowning slightly. He held a stoic demeanor, but the glint in his eyes betrayed his silence.

Edwards watched as Jeffreys shoved a knee into Bugs' stomach. Bugs crunched over, moaning.

I meant to say *"leave him alone!"* but all that came out was a squeal.

"That's enough now," Edwards scolded as he slapped handcuffs on Bugs. But it would take more than that to keep my mate under control.

Bugs stomped on Edwards' feet. "Sod off!" he yelled, his forehead cracking into my shoulder as he kicked.

"Look, just piss off and let him go!" I protested. The blood rose to my face, and my shoulder began to throb.

Jeffreys yelled out the door for backup. A couple more constables ran in and restrained Bugs, who was now trying to bite hands. He was rabid, his eyes black, his face jagged. Tony would have talked the cops out of taking us, as he usually did, but he was busy getting sick in the corner.

We were trapped. The police took us in for assault after Bugs' little outburst, not letting us make any calls. When they got sick of me screaming a rights scene, they agreed to send a message to my aunt that I was in custody.

In our cell, we scratched our names into the paint on the concrete walls until our fingers bled. Bugs had already kicked around for something to break, but I managed to get him to settle down a bit; it would be harder to convince Aunt Vi to get us out if we acted as angry as we felt.

"This is fucking bollocks," Bugs spat out, just loud enough that anyone around us could hear.

The warden peered over to our cell to make sure Bugs hadn't killed me or something since I had grown quiet, but it was because I was just sitting there, replaying the last night's scene through my mind. Miranda got her drugs from Gangrene, and, yeah, he was pretty low. But he was as poor as any of us, and these days you had to do whatever you could to make the rent. Those of us who weren't junkies eventually just ignored his job, and those who needed a fix knew where to go. That was it.

Bugs continued cursing next to me, working more holes into his battered t-shirt. I could hear him seething. The veins in his arms were still visible. *"You never fucking speak up, ya cunt,"* he'd always scold me. *"You never fucking throw a punch. You just stand there like a poof as the pigs take me in."*

I gritted my teeth, trying to push the thought out that Jeffreys could be right about the company I kept. *Some fucking good it did me doing it your way, Bugs.*

"I know what you're thinking," Bugs said, finally. "And you might as well forget about it." He flicked a paint chip across the hard floor. "You know she got what she deserved, the stupid tart."

I looked over at him, feeling strained.

"You can't save the world, mate. Hell, even if you could, it wouldn't be worth the bother." His boot struck the metal bars of the cell, sending a chilly echo throughout our small space.

A while later, a constable peeked his head around the cell and pointed. Edwards entered, followed by my plump, grey-haired aunt.

Aunt Violet frowned. "Yes, I am afraid this *is* my nephew." She looked through her dainty purse.

"Aunt Vi…"

She raised her hand to hush me without looking up. Then she pulled out a wad of fivers, which was quickly handed to Edwards. He said nothing, just took the money and placed it in his pocket discretely.

The warden let us out of the cell with no more than an accusing look.

"This is absolutely the *last* time I am coming here, Jonathan Alton Hunter," Aunt Vi scolded under her breath. She didn't even acknowledge Bugs.

Edwards followed us out of the station and waited there until we were in Aunt Vi's car and had driven away.

Aunt Vi fidgeted with the radio dials while she drove. Bugs rubbed his eyes, frowning. I turned to look out the window, not wanting to say a word.

"Oh, I do dislike stopping in this neighborhood," she said as we headed up Farringdon Road to get to my flat. Aunt Vi never stayed angry long, but by the way she was driving, it felt like she had one foot on the accelerator and the other on the brake.

"Really, Jonathan," Aunt Vi continued, "you should find yourself a proper job. Then you could move to Hillingdon. It's quite nice there, isn't it? You know, just yesterday Miriam Leese told me that her son relocated there, and that shopping was superb. Why they've even been talking about a new museum for a collection of Parisian paintings, and you *know* how much I love Paris. Miriam said…"

It was enough to drive a man mad.

But Aunt Vi meant well and, despite all the lengthy lectures, I knew that I could count on her if I was in trouble. That's where the line was drawn, though. She was my mother's older sister, a proper English woman who feared nothing except getting caught outside of her class. When I first came to London, my mother had arranged for her to take me in. My aunt was polite enough, but the journey ended with a wad of 10-pound notes and a hotel room until I found myself a flat. That was Aunt Vi.

"...and when he said '*no, darling, I meant the treacle, not the clotted cream,*' why, I just couldn't help but laugh aloud!"

Aunt Vi slammed on the brake and nearly sent me through the windshield, as I hadn't been paying attention. "Here we are, then. Now, do try and stay out of trouble. Really, Jonathan, I don't understand why you must always test the rules." She looked around quickly a few times.

"Thanks, Aunt Vi. But, really, Bugs and I didn't..."

Aunt Vi cut me off with a wave of her hand. "Now run along, dear."

As soon as we climbed out, she sped away, the door barely shut behind us.

"Well, I'm off, mate," Bugs said to me, rubbing his stomach.

"Why don't you stay a bit?" I offered. "You may as well."

Bugs shook his head. "Suz and Jules are supposed to be stopping by in a couple hours." He winked and elbowed me hard in the stomach.

It was as though he could care less about what just happened to us.

I trudged up the stairs alone to my flat, realizing on the third floor that I had forgotten my keys and hoping by the fourth floor that I hadn't locked the door. It was evening already; we had been at the station longer than I expected. And I was starving. Was there anything left in my kitchen? Whatever was in the fridge was as good as garbage; I couldn't count on the electricity having returned. And Mary. *Fuck!* I was supposed to meet with Mary!

The last flight is always the hardest. My body craved nicotine, and I envisioned the places where I could have left my cigarettes. I shook the door handle—it was locked. Jiggling it a little more didn't do the trick either, and I had nothing to pick the lock with.

Mary's going to be furious, I thought, sliding down against the door to sit on the floor. That was the way with her. Mary was usually quite easy to get along with, but she expected people to stick to their word.
When they didn't, there was hell to pay! Revenge was a real bitch, and Mary was a Scorpio, after all.

Just then, the lock clicked. I fell backwards as the door opened into my flat.

"Where the fuck have you been?" Mary asked. The gleam of a steak knife in her hand made my heart stop.

"I, uh…what the hell's that for?"

Mary looked at the knife and then blushed slightly. "Er... Just cooking supper. I've got some bangers 'n mash on."

I rolled over and got up, closing the door behind me.

"What's 'bangers and mash'?" I asked, peering over the kitchen counter at the stove.

"Sausage and potatoes, luv," she said as she scraped the bottom of the pan with the knife.

That seemed safe. I think Mary liked to tease me because we had less-colorful names for all this stuff back in the States.

"You're not really mad at me, are you?" I asked between bites, hoping to avoid an evening of passive-agressiveness.

Mary shook her head. "No, but you didn't answer my question."

When I told her about the call from Bugs and the trip to jail, she inadvertently dropped her fork. The tines caught the edge of her glass and tipped it over. Water spilled down off the corner of the table. The glass rolled onto its side, followed the stream of water, and shattered on the floor. It was dramatic and as if in slow-motion; we stared at the mess, wordless, for a few moments.

Mary started to apologize as I slid off my chair and knelt on the floor, using my fingers to brush the glass into a pile. She came down to help me, but as she leaned in, we cracked foreheads. Hand raised to her head, she fell back onto her bum, moaning. I did the same, but while trying to steady myself, my other hand fell into the pile of broken glass. Mary gasped when I held it up, blood pooling up in the creases on my palm. I hadn't felt a thing; the glass must have been razor-sharp. Blood dripped onto the floor, and Mary reached for anything remotely resembling a bandage.

The sting hit when I wiggled my fingers. Tears tingled in the corners of my eyes. I stifled a whimper.

"Oh God, Jon," Mary whispered, wrapping my hand as tightly as she could in a t-shirt. It was one I paid a small fortune for at Vivienne Westwood's shop.

"I'm alright, really," I replied and started cleaning up again. There was blood all around me, as the drips mingled with the puddle of water that began the whole mess.

We both had bruises on our foreheads. They were like twin birthmarks or war decorations. If Paul were here, we'd have compared whose were bigger or darker. But Mary just sat there staring at my mock-bandaged hand as though her eyes could get it to scab over.

"I've got it!" I said suddenly. "*Scabbed Over!*"

Mary's eyes broke from my wound, and a smile crept across her face. We were going over major points on her fanzine idea and had been trying to find a good title. She nodded at my choice, so that's what we went with. As for content, Mary liked the idea of reviewing the concerts we had seen and, since I worked in a record store, all the new punk singles that were being released. It was difficult to find articles and information on music and events that interested punks back then, so our fanzine could help fill that void. I also wanted to have the whole 'social commentary' thing as part of the zine, so Mary put me in charge of that. Keely would be keen on helping with that part as well. First up, the Queen's Silver Jubilee and the current state of the economy.

"What about something on Miranda?" Mary suggested.

I wrinkled my lips. Did I really want to write a story on that mess?

"It could be therapeutic," she offered. "Sort of."

I thought for a moment on it, feeling my brow furrow.

Mary's face softened. "Well, it's just an idea, anyway."

By the time I agreed to work on the story, my hand was numb. Mary had to head home for Keely, who was arriving tonight from Dublin, but she insisted I go to the hospital instead of escorting her the entire way.

We walked to the tube station together, and I made sure she got on the train before I left. On the way back to my flat, I stopped at the local hospital to have my hand repaired. The doctor looked at my wound like I did something illegal to get it. Antiseptic, stitches, and he was done, barely a word spoken. No matter, though, because as I was leaving, another sorry sod was on his way in, cursing and bleeding all over the waxed floor. There was something very familiar about it.

"*Bugs?*"

Tony looked up at me. He was trying his hardest to carry Bugs in, but our mate was proving too much to handle.

Seeing the blood, nurses ran over to help, and they whisked Bugs down a corridor into the casualty ward.

"What the hell happened?" I asked Tony, pulling him out of the way of a janitor who was trying to mop up the blood.

"Fucking Teddy cunts," Tony hissed. "What about you?" He nodded towards my cleanly-bandaged hand.

"Same here," I lied. "Out in full force tonight, I guess."

"Yeah, but we fucking got 'em this time, Jonny. We got 'em good."

Teddy Boys, they were called. They picked fights constantly with punks. It was a lot like the gang wars back home in the States, but with less fuss about turf and more fuss about damage. Teds looked like they came straight out of the 1950's, like James Dean only rougher—hair in quaffs, blue jeans cuffed, white t-shirts, black leather jackets. It was as much their uniform as rips and safety pins were ours.

I thought back to early last night, when we had gone to The Roxy. Boise Lou and his mates were a prominent group of Teds that seemed to really have it out for us. They were wandering Covent Garden, apparently anticipating that us punks wouldn't know that the Buzzcocks' show had been cancelled. Bugs was always ready for a spot of violence, but I snuck past, wanting only to have a few drinks with my mates after the tiring week I'd had.

Boise egged us on as we went into The Roxy. Bugs started getting riled up, but Tony pulled him through the doorway.

I stood in the shadow of the entrance and waited as Tony dragged Bugs towards the bar. Outside Boise was leaning against the front of the building, laughing. His mate Brody stood beside him like a little boy, silent and scared. Nige and Miranda passed, and Boise straightened up, following them until he got close enough to shove Nige from behind.

Miranda backed away into the street, yelling at Boise.

"Clear off, man! What do you want with me?" Nige asked in a forced American accent. His obsession with The Ramones made him an easy target.

I pressed myself close to the door, not wanting to leave my mate out there to fend for himself, but admittedly afraid of causing more of a distraction.

"A little bird tells me that you've been talking to my Harlowe," Boise hissed at him.

Nige backed off a bit, shaking his head.

"Why would he want her when he's got me?" Miranda scolded from the street. She slowly approached Nige, reaching for his arm to pull him away.

Boise lunged forward and snatched Miranda by the throat. She let out a tiny yelp and struggled in his grip. Miranda was thin from her habit and had less strength than she pretended she did.

Nige pushed Boise back, and tugged Miranda away when Boise let go of her. She held tight to Nige's arm, coughing to get her breath back.

Brody started to run for them, but Boise waved him off.

"You better be a little more careful, Coles. I've got you at the top of my list," Boise yelled out. He lit up a cigarette and leaned back against the building with Brody at his side.

I was still peering out at the street when Tony returned to me with Susan. Bugs created a scene near the bar and he was already bored, being that the show had been cancelled. Having seen what just transpired, I knew the evening's boredom would shift into an all-out war. By the look on my face, Tony could tell the action tonight would be *outside* The Roxy. He motioned to Bugs, and the guys all rushed back to the street to have a grand old time. I did my best to avoid the
confrontation and stay with the girls on the sidelines, but I still managed to get knocked around a bit.

Tony liked a good fight, and I learned by this time that if I didn't want any shit from him, I had to lie. Sure, I fought my battles when I needed to, but I wasn't like him and Bugs; I didn't go looking for trouble. *"It's when you get that first punch in, Jonny boy,"* Tony would say. *"You get a few of those cunts on the pavement, and they know you mean business. Otherwise, you might as well stay inside. If you can't run the streets, what good are you then?"*

So, I lied when I had to, and Tony watched my back.

At the hospital, I sat with Tony in the waiting area, wanting to get the update on Bugs. Tony was giving me a blow-by-blow recount of the fight, colorfully illustrated by his outrageous gestures.

"Then, out of nowhere, this little git ran up behind Bugs and cracked him one with a bat. A fucking cricket bat, mate! When I lunged at him, Boise Lou and a couple other Teddy cunts jumped me, punching me in the face..."

I eyed Tony as he continued, noting a barely-visible bruise on his face that appeared days' old and doubting a lot of what he said. Tony had a tendency to exaggerate in order to fit things into his wild conspiracy theories.

"...So I just gave it to them full-force. I kicked until they cleared off a bit, then scrambled for the bat. When I got it, I cracked the sodding thing to shreds on 'em. We're talking some splinters they'll never get out, mate! Won't be no more trouble tonight, Jonny!"

Tony smiled and patted my shoulder, looking quite chuffed.

"So, you two never got to see Susan and Julie?" I asked, wanting to change the subject.

"No, mate. Suz is taking us home, though.

She's off her shift soon. And she'll get Jules on the way back to the flat."

It hadn't even occurred to me how convenient this whole mess had become. Susan was a nursing assistant and was apparently on duty tonight.

"Well, I doubt Bugs is going to be in much of a snogging mood, Tony."

Tony shrugged. "Jules said she wasn't going to stay the night anyway."

That really wasn't particularly surprising to me; Julie spread herself around the scene just as much as Nige did. Still, I shrugged too and tried to sneak a cigarette as best as I could before I was thrown out.

Ten minutes later, Bugs came hobbling out to us, holding onto Susan's steady arm. The scene was surprisingly tender, considering how insane Bugs usually was. Susan must have been thinking the same thing because she gave me a kind smile, nodding slightly in understanding.

"He'll be alright," Susan replied. She stuffed a handful of pain pill packets into Tony's pocket. "Let's just get him out of here."

It was almost 1 a.m. when I arrived back at my flat. Susan sped off to get Julie, but I didn't see the point since Bugs was well-sedated in the back seat. He had been knocked around pretty good. His head was wrapped in gauze, both eyes were black and blue, another tooth was missing, and his middle was wound thick with bandages. No joy for him, that's for sure!

But, then, no joy for me either. Mary would be entertaining Keely, but I guess that's just as well since I had to work in the morning.

THREE

Fresh Slab Records was buzzing with business, and there wasn't enough room to move around. Mr. White, my boss, had debated whether or not he wanted to move the record shop into a King's Road storefront, but for now it was just a stall at the Beaufort Market, a building next to Vivienne Westwood's Seditionaries. Beaufort Market itself was like a big open shop that had been partitioned off into smaller areas, each of which were run by different merchants. Mostly, it was home to fashion stalls; we were the odd-guy-out. Fresh Slab occupied one of the larger spots off in a corner. Our stall was a more-or-less unfinished space made of pegboard and chain-link fencing, so we had to create our own shelves and displays.

My mate Paul was the only other employee, and between the two of us, we ran the shop. It was a disaster. I built the uneven wooden racks that held the records, while Paul worked on the music collection. Building that was hard at first because there weren't too many punk releases when Fresh Slab started. I had my brother Rick send over stuff from America that we couldn't get yet in England. Paul was Jamaican, and he added reggae to the mix. It didn't seem like something punks would like, but we did; the beats, the rebellion—it fit the bill just right. By this time in '77, though, bands were sprouting up after each Sex Pistols show, recording their own singles and marketing them to us. I had to build more racks, and space in our stand was getting tight.

Paul was late. It was already half past eleven, but he was nowhere to be seen. I had five impatient customers in the cramped space, no more bags, and a splitting headache. I wished Mr. White would hurry and move Fresh Slab into a proper shop, but he claimed he didn't have enough money. So, until then, I had to do what I could.

As I was coercing a young punk into buying a new single, the Stranglers display that Paul spent hours making came crashing down on us.

It was Gangrene.

"For fuck's sake, man!" I yelled at him.

Gangrene stepped over the mess, stumbling towards the sales counter.

I helped my newly-bruised customer up and got out of him a frightened and nervous sale, but a sale nonetheless.

"Jon, mate," Gangrene mumbled like nothing happened. "Can you lend me some cleanser?"

Huh? I wrinkled my nose at him. "The shop's down the street."

Gangrene repeated himself slowly, as if I didn't hear his request.

"What for, then?" I asked.

"We've got...uh...some business tonight, mate," he replied with a quick upward nod and a wink.

That should have been my clue right there to tell him to piss off, but someone was waiting behind him with a couple records in hand.

"Alright, here," I said, crouching down to grab the canister from beneath the counter. "But bring it back, mate. Don't make me answer to the boss."

Gangrene left with an *"oi!"* and a partially-toothless grin. And I made another five pounds.

Things died down by noon. Mary stopped in for a moment on her way to work, leaving me with some curry for lunch.

"You wouldn't be able to guess what time Susan came home," she said.

"I can imagine," I replied between bites. "Bugs said she and Julie were going over to their place."

"Yeah, well, I didn't expect her to actually spend the night." Mary looked a bit perturbed about it. "Do you really think she and Tony are that serious?"

I shrugged. "I never thought Tony would drop his guard to anyone, let alone someone as straight as Suz. What I can't understand, though, is how she can put up with him. Don't those guys upstairs make her nervous?"

"Hell, doesn't *Tony* make her nervous?" Mary asked. Her face showed genuine concern.

I gave her a long kiss to take her mind off of it and then watched her head down the road to the pub she worked at. She was in a bit of a mood because plans changed at the last minute; Keely wasn't able to make it to London. I admit being disappointed by that, too. My mates here were great, but Keely was the only one of our group that I could have any sort of intellectual discussion with. Well, *my* sort of intellectual discussion, that is. Paul and Mary were brilliant, but even they lacked patience in my existential ramblings over time. Maybe Keely just humored me out of respect for Mary, but even then, I appreciated her.

In between the occasional customer that afternoon, I tried setting up Paul's display again. Luckily, none of the records were damaged, but I couldn't figure out how Paul managed to keep his design standing upright. He built it out of a heavy cardboard carton that a shopkeeper upstairs didn't want. It was bent a few times here, scored and cut twice there, held together with gaffer tape, and spray-painted all over in orange. I was stumped.

I gave up on it to talk with a customer when Paul barged in.

"You won't believe this, mate," he panted, wiping his brow. "You won't bloody believe this." He was leaning on the counter as though he couldn't hold himself up.

I went to his side quickly. Paul wasn't one to exaggerate or over-react, but there he was, shaking and looking like he'd seen a ghost.

The customer stood there with me and listened like she was one of our mates.

"I was with Nige, right? And I was trying to get a ride to King's Road with him since I missed the train, yeah? So, he's telling me, right, that he'll drop me off here, no problem, but first I have to help him figure out what to do with Julie."

I peered at him curiously. The customer focused on every word Paul said.

"Well, I'm thinking, what the fuck does he need me to do that for, yeah? Tell her to go home, or stay, or whatever. But that's not it, right? I look into his bedroom, and there she is, on the floor all dead-like."

The customer shuddered. I felt my skin tense up and my heart rate increase. What was going on?

Paul's hand held tight to the counter. "I reached down and touched her...and she was cold, mate. I didn't know what to do. I just ran out of there and left him. Didn't stop til I got here." He wiped at his eyes with his forearm.

I offered him the rest of my coffee, though it was no longer warm. My hand began to shake, enough that I could barely pass the cup to him without spilling it.

"Her fucking eyes were open, mate," he whispered, his whole body shivering. "She was set out all stiff. And Nige was just standing there...like nothing. Like fucking nothing, Jon."

Paul's story got us ten quid from the customer before she slipped out, thoroughly distraught. I didn't know what to say to him.

"Did you hear about Miranda, then?" I felt the words escape my lips before I could stop them.

Paul shook his head. "Now what did she do?"

"She overdosed after we left the party."

"That tart needs to get herself together."

"No, I mean, she's dead."

Paul said nothing to that, just leaned against the pegboard wall of our stall. He finished off the rest of my coffee and then crumpled the cup, tossing it at the dustbin but missing.

I stared at the crushed paper for a few moments before picking it up.

"I think I could use a pint," Paul finally said.

I agreed.

We decided to close up early and didn't even care if Mr. White found out.

"What the hell happened here?" Paul pointed at what was previously his Stranglers display as we were leaving.

"Gangrene."

He frowned slightly. "*Bastard.* It took me five hours to put that thing together!"

Paul briefly inspected my repair job, his forehead wrinkling as he calculated the adjustments he'd surely have to make. "It can wait," he sighed.

McSurley's Pub was a bit displaced on King's Road, wedged between a couple artsy clothing shops. Inside, it was like any proper Irish pub, down to the warm wood surfaces. The bloke who owned it was an old friend of Mary's grandmother, a round, callus-handed man named Seamus. He was known for giving out rounds on good days, and I prayed that today was one.

Mary saw Paul and me slump against the bar, and she approached.

"Are you two working bankers' hours today, then?" She winked at me and wiped down the counter in front of us, seemingly in a better mood than when I saw her a few hours earlier.

I didn't want to ruin the moment, but it couldn't be helped. "I think we need some pints, Maire," I said, the lowness of my voice vibrating through my own chest.

"There's some pork pies cooled in back," Mary offered, pulling us two glasses of Guinness.

Paul shook his head solemnly.

The smile that warmed Mary's face faded. "What's going on?"

"Julie's dead," Paul replied softly, his gaze riveted on the heavy head of his drink.

"*What?!*" Mary's voice was loud and shrill.

Behind us I heard chairs creak.

Mary softened and leaned in closer to us. "What are you talking about?" she whispered anxiously.

Paul gave her an abbreviated version of the story. I sat and drank my pint, trying to get the taste of disgust out of my mouth.

Fucking junkies, I cursed to myself. And Miranda and Julie weren't the only ones. I wanted to shake them all, ask them what the hell they were doing. How do you change the world when you're not even in it? How can you stand for something when you're just a statistic? Bugs teased at my sincerity if I said anything aloud, but it ate me up inside. Tony called it a 'Christ Complex,' and he had a theory about it, just like everything else: *"You want to save the world, Jonny. All you fucking Americans do. Big Brother, mate. Sodding Big Brother tells you the world needs you, and then you've got hope. Well, it's time to wake up. This ain't bloody America."*

"I guess I can't really say I'm all that surprised," said Paul. He and Mary had continued their conversation while my mind drifted.

"Well, all I'm saying is that it seems odd," Mary replied.

Paul shrugged. "When you use junk, it can happen."

"But doesn't it seem strange that it's Miranda and Julie this week, when just a fortnight ago Tommy from Crawley got done in?"

"I thought Teds got him, Maire," I interjected. Tommy was an irritating little prick with a mouth that never stopped. It was only a matter of time that a Ted shut him up permanently, so I wasn't shocked to hear that the police found his battered body stuffed in a skip at the tube station.

Mary shook her head. "Overdose. That's what Suz said. She thought it was odd even then, before Miranda."

"An overdose?" Paul questioned, almost mockingly in his disbelief. "Why would he overdose in Sloane Square? With Teds around on a Saturday night, at that! She must be thinking of some other sorry sod."

Paul and Mary went back and forth a while more until business began to pick up. When Mary had her hands full with customers, Paul and I decided we would make the dreaded trip to tell Susan.

"Maybe there's just purer junk on the street now?" Paul suggested on the train to King's Cross. What Mary said must have gotten to him.

I shrugged. "Look, Tony can give us the latest conspiracy theory on this one. It's probably all just a coincidence. I mean, between junkies and Teds, what can you expect?"

Paul nodded to that, and we rode the rest of the way in silence.

Getting off the tube at King's Cross was no easy task that evening, as far as our hearts were concerned. The area itself was more a red light district than a neighborhood, but even that paled in comparison to the job Paul and I had awaiting us. Outside the girls' apartment, Paul and I tossed a coin to determine who would break the news to Susan. Paul was so nervous that he dropped it a couple times before I officially lost. I tried to psych myself out, but I was nervous, too.

Paul knocked on the door, and we waited. He knocked again, and we waited longer.

"Maybe she left for her shift already."

I listened in. "Nah," I said softly. "Mary said she wasn't scheduled tonight."

Paul fidgeted, looking around the stairwell repeatedly.

Deep within the room I could hear a sound like that of sobs, muffled through the plaster walls.

"Come on, Paul." I pulled my ear from the door. "She already knows."

I was relieved to awake the next morning to the lonely sound of my clock—no frantic telephone calls, no breathless discoveries. Just my safe bed, the trusty bleating of the alarm, and a faint snoring coming from Paul who had spent the night buried somewhere in my couch.

Both the stove and sink were working, so I took advantage of the situation and put tea on. Paul snored away, softly at first, then louder as he moved in his sleep. An afghan my grandmother gave me was wrapped tightly around his legs but dangled off his chest and onto the floor, collecting dust that I hadn't hoovered.

I sat and smoked a cigarette, waiting for the kettle to whistle its way to a nice cup of tea. Paul stirred a little, then the white of one eye was visible. The eye looked around for a moment before settling on my smoky form at the kitchen counter.

"I thought I was having a bad dream," Paul grumbled, waking up. "But now I know it's real."

I smirked. "Look, I cleaned last week, man! I can't help that you missed it!"

Paul let out a gravelly chuckle from within the cushions, and I took a heavy drag on my cigarette, watching him pull himself out of the afghan's grasp. We had another long day ahead of us. The thought of spending it all in a garage-sized space at Beaufort Market made me wish I put a bottle of vodka out for breakfast instead. But Paul was softly singing his usual Johnny Clarke tune with the sun peeking through the heavy smog, and that feeling of hope washed over me again.

≠

"Do you think Mr. White's ever going to fill Billy's order?"

Paul was rifling through receipts, trying to figure out why we were missing a whole section of records but discovering new problems.

"I doubt it," I replied, wiping down the counter with water since Gangrene had taken all of our cleanser. "He did the same thing a few months back with Nige's stuff. I had to get Rick to send it instead." My brother did more work for Fresh Slab from back in the States than Mr. White did, and for free yet.

"Speaking of which," Paul said, "do you have that Max's Kansas City record he sent?"

I nodded and rummaged around for it. Once located, I put it on the record player and cranked up the volume. "Good stuff, huh?"

"Those blokes in Pere Ubu are brilliant, mate," Paul replied.

"Yeah, I got to see them play a few times back home. One of those perks when they're from your hometown, you know?" I smiled proudly, as if I could claim some type of great lineage. Still, we had some great bands in Cleveland: Pere Ubu, the Dead Boys, and the Electric Eels, to name just a few. It was even the seemingly ignored spirit of the Electric Eels that exposed me to the "look" of punk; they had that '*I don't care*' style that said you could wear whatever the fuck you wanted, however the fuck you wanted, and wherever the fuck you wanted. My parents weren't so convinced, but I knew the Eels had something going for them.

Paul threw down a stack of receipts and an annoyed sigh escaped from his lips. "Why does he do this shit? I wish we owned this place."

"One of these days, Paul. As soon as I can get my hands on the kind of cash it'll take, I'll toss around the idea with him."

"Marla thinks he's just mucking around anyway."

That was true. Mr. White's wife had been nagging him ever since I started working there (perhaps even before) to sell off the business. He owned a couple launderettes near Paul's flat in Brixton and made enough money from them to stay home and do nothing all day long. Paul and I theorized that the record store was his mid-life crisis acquisition, an attempt at staying young and hip.

"If it weren't for us, Fresh Slab would go under in a second! What the fuck does that cunt know about this business?"

Paul agreed. "All he cares about is this." He held up the pile of receipts he had been going through.

As if on cue, a new batch of customers arrived, keeping us busy until mid-afternoon. Between sales, Paul and I snacked on yesterday's pork pies that Mary dropped off during a break from McSurley's. The food made us lethargic and nearly oblivious to the noise outside the Market.

Nearly.

"I know there's a recession, but, damn... doesn't anyone in this city work anymore?" Paul asked, peering out of the shop and hoping to catch a glimpse of the commotion through the glass doors of Beaufort Market.

I sat on the floor, full and propped up by one of the record stands.

"You mean like us?" I chuckled, not about to move to see what he was looking at.

He laughed his hearty laugh and tried to be more productive by repairing his Stranglers display.

I got only as far as changing the album on the record player to one of Paul's reggae selections; I was too knackered to do anything else.

Paul swayed a bit to the beats, singing along, not even noticing an awkward Susan approaching.

"Suz, hey, how are you doing?" I managed to ask before being overcome by a long yawn.

Susan looked worn, but was otherwise calm and collected.

Paul turned when I spoke, taking Susan's hands in his and moving her around to the music. She smiled gently and followed his lead before heading into our stall.

"Are you working tonight?" Paul asked, putting an arm around her.

Susan shook her head. "No, I'm not up for it. I asked for a couple days holiday." She smiled again, but uncomfortably, like she was fighting back a deep frown.

"So, what brings you out here?" Paul brushed loose strands of long brown hair away from her face.

"I just thought I'd do some window-shopping."

"And be with friends," I offered.

Susan's face softened a bit, and she nodded.

"Well, it's a good thing you stopped by," Paul added, "because that binder over there is too useless to help me fix up the place."

Susan giggled at me slumped on the floor.

"Yeah, yeah, I see how it is. Go ahead, joke at my expense," I teased.

Paul went back to working on his display and Susan helped, which was a pretty damn good idea on Paul's part since it might get her mind off of Julie.

When they were finished, they joined me on the floor. The early day's traffic didn't return the rest of the afternoon, so we all lounged around. I thought about the singles I'd review for the zine while Paul tested new music out on Susan. She admitted that she liked The Ramones and the reggae that he put on, but she wrinkled her face at most of my picks.

"I'm just too hard for you," I joked.

Susan chuckled. "Like all the Teds outside?"

"Is that what all the noise is?" Paul asked.

Susan nodded. "They're coming out of the woodwork today. Must be a show or something tonight. Good thing I'm not a punk, then."

Paul laughed. "See? You're fine just the way you are. Better, even. You don't have to get shoved around like us sorry sods."

I ran my hand through my cropped hair. "I just knew today couldn't be as calm as I hoped."

Susan was lucky she didn't wear the increasingly familiar punk 'uniform'. It made her less conspicuous. But she couldn't be too careful, though. Guilt by association. Punks and Teds followed that rule by the book.

We chatted for an hour or so more before Susan got up to leave.

"I'm going to head to the pub for a bit before I go back to the flat. If you aren't doing anything tonight, why not stop by?"

She looked like she could still use some friends. And we'd be there for her.

Paul and I closed the shop around 8 p.m. The nearest tube station, Sloane Square, was a bit of a walk from Beaufort Market. We were cautious with the warning that Susan gave us, but the street seemed strangely quiet. Too quiet for King's Road, Teds or no Teds.

As we were nearing the station, a bottle rolled out from an alley one building ahead of us. We slowed down, and I reached in my pocket for the switchblade I carried with me. Paul stayed close behind. We prepared to run as we reached the alley, but stopped once we saw what it was.

FOUR

"Suz!" Paul called out.

We ran over to her. What was she doing laying in the gutter?

I looked around briskly. The section of the street around us was motionless, and the alley was empty save for Susan's crumpled self.

"Are you alright?" Paul was kneeling on the pavement, stroking Susan's forehead.

She was propped up against the wall. Her hair was tousled and her cheeks looked bruised or flushed; I couldn't tell which.

"Who did this to you?" I asked, crouching down to her. There was blood starting to trickle down the corner of her mouth. Whatever happened, it couldn't have been more than a few moments ago. Yet, Paul and I didn't hear a thing.

Susan gasped, her eyes not focusing on anything, her pupils mere points.

"Stay with us, Suz," Paul whispered nervously.

"Paul, go ring the police. And tell Mary. I'll stay with her."

Paul nodded and ran off quickly.

I kept my fingers at her neck, feeling her pulse. It was slow and faint.

A streetlight flickered on belatedly. Something sparkled beside her. I looked over. There was a syringe on the ground. Susan didn't shoot drugs, that I knew for sure. She drank a bit, but other than that she was clean. In fact, she was more adamant about not using drugs than anyone I knew. Working at the hospital, she never hesitated to lecture the junkies among us about the dangers of their addictions.

But here she was, slumped over in King's Road, apparently strung out and fading fast.

"Hang on, Suz. Paul went for help. And I'm here with you. Just hang on, luv."

I held her close to me. Lifesaving was not something I had learned. I guessed at what to do or check for. She still had a pulse, though it felt very light and erratic. When I put my hand to her mouth, I could barely feel the heat of her breath. In my head pounded the mantra *please don't die, please don't die, please don't die*. Fear rose through me so thoroughly I couldn't even piss my pants.

When I finally heard the sirens, I was relieved. Susan was barely with me, and I never thought I would ever look forward to seeing the police.

I waved frantically to the paramedics that followed. They piled out of the ambulance with various supplies; Paul relayed the message well. I was utterly helpless at the scene, watching the men check out her eyes, her vitals. She couldn't move by herself. Her face was stone, and she was silent. I could feel the blood pulsing through my veins, so I concentrated on it, not even hearing Edwards approach me from behind.

His hand firmly grasped my shoulder, shaking me from my shock.

"So, Mr. Hunter, we meet again."

Jeffreys wasn't there to back him up, but I couldn't have fought back even if I wanted to.

A couple paramedics brought out a stretcher and carefully lifted Susan onto it. She twitched slightly, but her eyes didn't move. It was like she was staring straight at me, burning a hole right through my forehead for letting this happen.

As Susan was loaded into the ambulance, a police car stopped at the scene. Jeffreys exited, while another constable remained in the driver's seat.

"Looks like you beat us to it, Chief Inspector," Jeffreys said, watching the ambulance speed away.

Chief Inspector?

I stood there like an idiot, not sure what to do.

Edwards nodded. "I got here as quickly as I could."

"What's the story, then?" Jeffreys asked.

"It looks like another drug overdose. Radio in to the station that it's under control. We'll follow up with the hospital."

Jeffreys nodded and hurried back to the police car, reiterating the information to the operator at the station.

"But...it *can't* be an overdose!" I stammered.

Jeffreys looked up at me from the car.

Edwards stood calm and collected, but his face showed a tinge of something that seemed to say I was just making a simple routine difficult.

"Do you know something we don't?" Jeffreys asked, returning to Edwards' side.

"I know she didn't use drugs, that's for sure!"

"Yeah? Well it's a bit curious that you happen to be at another crime scene..."

Edwards held his hand up to Jeffreys, interrupting his intended accusatory speech. "Perhaps you ought to come with us, Mr. Hunter."

Jeffreys seethed beside Edwards, looking as though tossing me in jail and throwing away the key would have made the evening a hell of a lot more enjoyable than interviewing me.

In shock, and against my better judgment, I climbed into the police car and went along to the station.

Jeffreys handed me a cigarette. I was sitting in a concrete-grey windowless room, bathed by the pure white light that hung from the ceiling. Nervous as hell, I sucked down smoke as soon as Jeffreys gave me a light.

Edwards sat down across from me and spoke slowly. "So, Mr. Hunter, you have some ideas on this case?"

I studied him for a moment. His face was blank, bored. He couldn't have been much older than my own father, but his hair was already silver.

Shivering, I took a drag from my cigarette. Jeffreys stood at my side, chewing on his pen.

"Look, all I'm saying is that Susan doesn't do drugs. She's clean."

"Are you certain of that?" Edwards asked unflinchingly. His voice came off as though trying a little too hard not to be scathing. He must have noticed that himself because he relaxed a bit then, softening to compensate for the tone.

I nodded, coughing on smoke. "I've known her since I moved here. She doesn't associate with junkies, man."

Jeffreys' brow furrowed in thought. He took the pen out of his mouth as if he were going to ask something, but Edwards continued.

"And what is your relationship to Miss Bowman?"

"She's a friend. My girlfriend's flatmate."

"Then if she's your friend, there's no need to lie to us, Mr. Hunter."

I peered at him. "What?"

"Covering up her drug use won't help her," Edwards replied gently.

"But, I'm not!" I spat out, agitated and rising

from the seat. "I told you she's not a junkie!"

Jeffreys put a hand on my shoulder and eased me back down. "When was the last time you saw her?" His voice was cold, clearly not believing me.

I shrugged him away. "Just a few hours before I found her in the alley. She stopped to see me while I was working."

"You work on King's Road then, Mr. Hunter?"

I nodded, taking another drag on my cigarette. The words *Beaufort Market* followed dumbly. I could hear Jeffreys chewing away on his pen, exhaling through his nose like someone who had just run a marathon.

Edwards reached up and scratched his cheek. The light glinted for a quick moment off one of his eyes.

"And what was her state of mind when you last saw her?" he asked.

"She was upset..."

As I explained what the situation was, it became clear to me that it was a prompt. I was cornered into agreeing that Susan had a motive for shooting up, as crazy as it may be.

A constable stuck his head into the room and motioned to Jeffreys. Edwards wrote something down in his notepad, the first note I saw him take all night.

Jeffreys frowned and tossed his gnarled pen in a rubbish bin.

"That was the hospital. I'm afraid your friend didn't make it."

The words hit me like a brick to the chest and a shiver spread throughout my limbs. I'm sure my eyes looked like they'd burst out of their sockets.

Susan was gone? No. No, this couldn't be happening.

My cigarette turned to ash as my mind (and heart) raced.

There was silence for a few moments. Then Jeffreys lit another one for me. My hands were clammy and the paper of the cigarette stuck to my fingers, ensuring that I wouldn't drop it in my shock. I could feel the warm flush of a panic attack coming on.

He pulled up a chair and sat at the side of the table, between Edwards and me.

"We think these deaths are the result of a recent drug acquisition," Jeffreys said bluntly, breaking the silence.

"And we believe one Daniel Green is involved," Edwards added.

I blinked.

"Yes, we know you're a mate of his." Edwards spoke softly, but never broke his gaze from my face.

My cigarette was now an oxygen tank, and I inhaled desperately. This had to be a nightmare. Any second I'd wake up sweaty and breathless, but safe in my own room with my own shadows.

Yet they continued.

"We want you to watch him. If he does anything unusual, we want to know," Jeffreys said.

I agreed wordlessly, intent on one thing only—crawling into my bed and sleeping until I couldn't remember this night.

Edwards had me driven to my flat in a big black area car. Jeffreys sat in the rear seat beside me, murdering a new pen between his teeth.

"Lovely," Jeffreys said sarcastically as we pulled up to my council block, his glistening pen pointing at the building.

I frowned.

Edwards leaned back in the passenger's seat as I got out of the car. "Try to get some rest now," he said, fatherly.

"We'll be in touch," Jeffreys added with a smirk.

Mary was curled up in my couch, asleep. Her breath was soft but muffled, as she was almost completely enveloped by the cushions. There were bills lying on my kitchen counter from the second delivery, and the checklist in my head of all the things I had to do or worry about was sizzling. But I was totally exhausted.

Sleep. I needed sleep.

Yet, I reached for the phone. I had to call Paul first. It was well past midnight on a work night, and I hoped he was still conscious.

Paul answered on the third ring. His voice sounded distant, filtered.

"She's gone, mate," he said plainly.

"They told me at the station," I whispered, partly because I didn't want to wake Mary and partly because my voice was cracking.

"Is Mary there?"

"Yeah, she's sleeping."

"She took it hard, mate." Paul cleared his throat.

We decided to finish the conversation later, and I could hear him sniffling as I hung up the phone.

I gathered Mary up in my arms, trying my best not to jolt her awake, and trudged to the bedroom. She moaned after I lost my grip, accidentally flopping her onto the bed.

"Sorry, Maire," I mouthed.

Her eyelids opened heavily, and she stretched. "Jon..."

I bent over a bit, pulling off and tossing my clothes to the floor. "Yeah?" I could feel that my voice was tired.

Mary didn't answer. When I turned back toward the bed, I saw that she had fallen asleep again. I undressed her as best I could, climbed in next to her, and buried my face in her hair to muffle my sobs.

≠

"What's happening to us, Jon?" Mary asked, wiping her eyes. She was crunched up on the side of my bed, her legs dangling.

My heart was heavy this morning. I had been chain-smoking for the last three hours, watching Mary sleep since I hadn't been able to do so myself. Her lithe body shivered every 15 minutes, as though it were trying to wake her from an awful dream. She'd move her head from side to side, mouthing pleas or prayers; I couldn't tell which. Her eyes stayed closed, glued shut by tears. Knowing her as I did, I wanted to be the one man in her life that wouldn't disappoint her, but in this I was helpless. I couldn't save Susan, and I had no idea if we were in danger ourselves.

"I'm so scared," she wept, her face in her hands. I had never seen her this vulnerable before. She was always the ungrounded, unbridled, untouchable one. But now, the sheets were bunched around her waist in a twisted pile, keeping her steady as her body shuddered between sobs. Her black hair hung limply.

"I'll stay with you tonight, Maire," I offered. "Or I'll give you the money to go to Caoilinn. Whatever you need."

I pulled her close, resting my chin on the top of her head. She felt so tiny at that moment, cradled in my arms like a child. Her fear bled through me and made my insides quiver. Feeling another panic attack coming on, I took long, slow drags on my cigarette to compensate.

Mr. White was not thrilled when I skived work. Paul had apparently phoned him earlier doing the same, and now Mr. White had to run the shop today on his own. He was being inconvenienced, but I didn't care. Let the tosser see what it's like to be in that little space all day long, alone. Let him see what he really got himself into. He thought he was following in Malcolm McLaren's footsteps, but he had no idea.

I gritted my teeth for a moment, then tried to relax. Death does funny things to those left behind. Anger and fear coexisted inside me. I could barely think straight or stop shaking. Mary wasn't the only one of us who was scared.

"We'll get everything together, Maire. I'll ring the guys to move stuff around, if you want. It'll be okay, luv."

Mary nodded as we walked to her flat, but said nothing. She was dreading the return home like someone just widowed, and I couldn't blame her. Pretty much everything in their place had been Susan's.

As we walked up the stairs in her building, voices filled the hallway. Mary looked up, apparently recognizing the sounds. I peeked into the doorway and saw a few blokes my age along with an older man who looked to be Susan's father. They were in Susan's bedroom hurriedly packing boxes to overflowing with her things and moving furniture. Mary squeezed past me and headed towards them.

"Mr. Bowman, I…" she started softly, but stopped when he turned around.

Susan's father glared at Mary as though she were responsible for what had happened.

"How *dare* you," he seethed. "Have you no conscience?"

The other guys there continued to work but quickened their pace even more. Mary's eyes trembled.

"You're murderers, getting her involved in all that rubbish. You're murderers, the lot of you!"

Mary stood there and wept aloud. I started to argue with Susan's father, pulling Mary close to me, but nothing I could say would matter now. It was then, with his eyes slicing through me, that I knew it was up to me to find the answer to this deadly puzzle. For Susan and the rest of us.

They emptied the apartment, taking everything except what Mary owned—which amounted to her clothes, some records, and a few trinkets saved from her late parents. So much for sorting through Susan's stuff.

While Mary sat on the floor trying to compose herself, I took a quick survey. If I could get Paul here, all three of us could toss her things into a cab and drop everything off at my place. Maybe that was too simple an answer, but I knew Mary couldn't afford to stay in her flat on her own. She didn't make much money at the pub and her landlord had raised the rent yet again this past spring. And with Susan's things gone, there was barely enough furniture for a prison cell.

I figured Mary wouldn't go for my idea as she usually had the upper hand, but she agreed without argument. Guilt panged inside me a little knowing that I had ultimately made the decision for her, but I couldn't stew over that now; we needed to pick ourselves up and keep moving. So Mary started piling up her things while I ran down to the phone box on the corner to have Paul come with a cab.

But Paul had news of his own.

"Tony went fucking bollocks last night, mate. And when I rang there this morning, Bugs said that Susan's family would have us escorted out if we showed up at the funeral."

My jaw clenched for a moment.

"This is a bloody nightmare," Paul sighed. There was a momentary silence, and he finished: "I'll be on my way, then."

When he hung up, I quickly dialed Keely, asking the operator to reverse the charges. I prayed Keely would accept the call.

"Jon, luv," she answered nervously. "Is Maire all right?"

I gave her a 30-second summary of the day's events, which left her understandably upset. Susan was her friend as well; it was through Keely that Mary and Susan met, after all. Keely seemed to have her own emergency in Dublin, however. I could hear a commotion on the other end, made noisier by a panicked news report on the telly. She wouldn't say what was going on, only that she didn't know how soon she could arrive in London. It was up to me to sort things out.

When we finally arrived back at my flat, it was inching towards evening. I could hear my phone ringing through the door and I rushed to get it, dropping some of Mary's clothes in the process. Bugs was on the other end mumbling something about the three of us coming over for drinks. From what I could hear in the background, it sounded like he could use some saner company.

"I'm tellin' ya what it is, Jonny boy," Tony said as he held onto my shirt. "That fuckin' cunt Nige. We'll get something on him."

Bugs had gotten Tony on a regimen of whiskey shots in an attempt to calm him down, and now he could barely stand.

"Oh, bollocks!" Bugs yelled from the kitchen. "What the fuck would Nige have to do with anything?" He coughed a bit, holding his side. The bandages were off of his head, but I could still see some bunched underneath his shirt. His face was beginning to heal from the bruises he sustained in the fight the other night. Paul rushed to his side upon arriving to better view the multi-hued damage, and so they were both in the kitchen where the light was brightest.

"So, what makes you think Nige is involved?" I asked Tony, whispering a bit so that Bugs wouldn't hear. My hand gripped Tony's shoulder to help him remain upright.

Tony looked from side to side slowly as if preparing to tell me a deep secret, losing his balance a bit as he did so. He leaned in towards me and with his stale, alcoholic breath mumbled: "He's a player, Jonny boy. Spread across the green as far as you can see, the cunt."

So that was it? Not much of a secret there. Nige definitely had his way with the ladies; that was an obvious fact.

I eyed Tony curiously. Was he implying that Nige's trysts were something more? What did he know about the situation that the rest of us didn't?

Tony plopped down on a chair. "First Miranda. Then Jules," he replied as if telepathic.

"But...what would he get from it?"

"First Miranda. Then..."

Tony's eyes closed slowly as he slumped back, mouth open. I frowned, but he needed to sleep after a day like this. So I left him there and joined the others in the kitchen.

"Maybe Tony's got a point," I said as we tossed out our theories.

Bugs shook his head. "Don't start falling for that git's answer to this mess. First it's Nige, then he'll get going into how the pigs are working a bloody cover-up on the whole thing...as if they'd even bother! What's a few punks to them?"

"They're not much help right now, though," Mary interjected.

"Well, when are they?" Bugs responded sharply. "Those wankers aren't clever enough to get away with something like this anyway."

"They told me that they've got their eyes on Gangrene. That he's cutting it with some shit, or it's a stronger drug out now," I said.

Bugs shrugged.

"That might explain Miranda and Julie, but it sure as hell doesn't fit for Susan!" Paul's voice grew excitedly.

"Sure it could," Bugs argued. "He could have finally had enough of her nagging about his 'job' and took care of the problem."

Wow. Could Gangrene really have gone that far?

Mary frowned.

"There's got to be something better than that," Paul replied. He shook his head in disbelief. "Teds, maybe."

I agreed. "She came in earlier and even said that the streets were full of them."

"Like Tommy, you mean?" Bugs asked.

Paul nodded.

Bugs thought about that for a moment, and nodded as well.

"Something's just not right," Mary said. "Why Susan? Why not one of us, then? We're more visible than she was."

"Then maybe it's just random violence. I mean, that's not unheard-of around here," I replied.

Bugs smirked.

Tony's loud snoring from the other room slowly ended our conversation. By the time we left, I had my mind looking into the genuine possibility that Teds were involved, and I worried how I'd go about solving this crime.

≠

"What if the pigs are right? What if it *is* Gangrene?" Paul asked the next morning. He was adding to his Stranglers display before the first customers arrived at the shop.

I was trying to re-alphabetize the records. "I guess he's got a motive...but I think it's a really weak one."

Paul stacked the few copies we had left of *Ratus Norvegicus* on his handmade shelves. We were preparing for the release of the new single in a few days and somewhat bracing for the worst since the album had surprisingly (at least to me) sold so quickly. Our little stall couldn't handle another rush of traffic like that.

"I just don't know what to think," Paul said, shaking his head. He stepped away from the display to view his repair. "But we need to find out what's going on, mate. It's starting to hit too close."

Paul rubbed his eyes with the heels of his hands. He sighed aloud and looked out to the next stall, which sold '50's-style clothes.

"Have you seen Nige lately?" I asked, my fingers reading the edges of the record sleeves, risking cuts from the low-budget cardboard.

"Not since Julie died. Something tells me to keep away from him."

I gave a quick nod. Paul came over and lent me a hand. His fingers were deft, and he did the job in half the time I could, with half the injuries.

"Mary told me about the zine, mate. Brilliant!"

I smiled. "She wants to work on it tonight. Why don't you come along?"

"Can't. Got a date with the bint across the way." He motioned to the stall his gaze had been at moments before.

"Next time then, eh?" I suggested.

As Paul nodded, in hobbled Bugs, looking as disheveled as ever.

He pushed a browser out of the way as he approached us. "Did you know that Gangrene is waving a pistol around out front?"

FIVE

"Well, get him the fuck out of here, then!" I scowled.

Bugs smirked and lit up a cigarette. He leaned against a shelf, taking a slow drag, not moving.

Paul tugged at my sleeve and nodded towards the door.

I clenched my teeth so tightly that it felt as though they could crack at any moment. *Bastard.*

Bugs wasn't lying; Gangrene certainly was out front waving around a gun.

"Piss off, ya bastards! Ya fuckin' Teddy cunts!" he yelled insanely.

The people who were on King's Road at the time rushed nervously into the shops they were nearest to, but I was in even more of a panic; I didn't need the pigs here.

Paul tried to coax Gangrene inside. Gangrene was flailing his arms, finger still on the trigger.

"Fuckin' stop, Green!" I yelled, reaching for him while trying to dodge the moving weapon.

"Come on, mate," Paul suggested in an attempt to calm him down. "Let's just go inside for a bit, okay?" He took hold of Gangrene's arm.

Gangrene struggled and tried to pull away, but I could see that Paul's grip tightened.

"Ya think ya got me, bloody Teds. Ya think ya fuckin' got me..."

I nodded to Paul and motioned for him to hold Gangrene's arm from a slight distance. Paul looked at me then at my right arm which I pulled back slowly.

"I'll blow all your fuckin'..."

—POW!—

My fist cracked into Gangrene's jaw with all the force I could muster. He stumbled back a couple steps, dropping the gun. Paul let go of his arm, and Gangrene crumpled over onto the pavement.

"Fucking cunt," I whimpered, holding my hand. My knuckles felt broken.

Paul gave Gangrene a good kick in the ass. No groan, no movement; he was out.

"Grab the pistol, Jon. I'll drag him inside."

I picked the gun up and went to open the door for Paul. Bugs was standing there on the other side, composing himself after an apparent fit of laughter.

When I propped the door open, Bugs flicked his cigarette to the ground, not even bothering to stomp it out.

"That was the most hilarious thing I've ever seen!" he laughed.

"Bloody help me, mate," Paul panted. He was tugging at Gangrene's arms, trying to pull him towards the door. Gangrene's body was like rubber, stretching but not moving.

Bugs smirked. He picked up Gangrene's feet half-assedly and managed to help Paul carry the body into the building. I held the door open with my back, looking around obsessively to make sure no cops were heading our way. People were slowly starting to return to the street.

Inside Beaufort Market, Paul, Bugs, and I dragged Gangrene beside our stall.

"I wonder what that was all about?" Paul exhaled as he wiped at his forehead.

I kicked Gangrene's leg. "Arsehole."

Bugs leaned against the Stranglers display, lighting up another cigarette.

"How's Tony doing, then?" I asked.

He shook his head, smoke streaming out of his mouth. "He's gone spazzy. Suz was the limit. I just had to leave for a bit. If I hear one more conspiracy theory...I think I'll shoot myself in the head, mate!"

That reminded me—the gun! I had shoved the damn thing in my pocket during the rush to get inside.

Bugs saw me reach for it, and he held his hands up, chuckling. "I didn't say I wanted to do it *right now!*"

I smirked, aiming it at him playfully.

"Hey, empty the thing first before you do that, mate!" Paul cringed and cowered.

"Oh...right! Sorry!" I turned the gun over in my hand and inspected it. How the hell did you open one of these anyway?

"Give me that, you poof," Bugs snorted, snatching the gun away from me. He cocked it to the side, rolled the barrel, and shook. Nothing came out.

Bugs cackled.

I should have guessed it wouldn't be loaded.

"Well, that's Gangrene, innit?" Bugs chuckled some more.

Paul smiled and relaxed a bit. "Are you going to be here til closing, Jon?"

I nodded. "You can cut out early if you want. Go get ready for your date, man!"

Bugs nudged Paul playfully. Paul retaliated with a quick jab to the gut. To that, Bugs let out a pained cry, ribs still healing.

"Right, then," Bugs coughed. "I think I'll go hit the pubs a bit."

Paul and Bugs went their separate ways, leaving me with Gangrene who was beginning to regain consciousness. His moaning echoed from the corner, weaving its way into all the stalls on the first floor of the building. A few heads popped out, looking for the source of the sound.

Gangrene's eyes opened heavily. He

reached a hand up to his jaw. "What the bloody hell did you do that for, mate?" he asked, speech slurred.

"Well, what the fuck were you doing out there with a gun, you stupid git? You could have had the pigs here!"

Gangrene tried to sit up. "What?" He looked at me like I was speaking another language. "I was just out for a pint, mate! If you wanted a fight, you should have grabbed for a Ted, not me!"

"A pint?! Before or after all the junk you took? You were fucking insane, Green! Waving a gun around in broad daylight? What are you on?"

"Me? What are *you* on, mate? I don't even own a pistol!"

This guy was unbelievable. How could he have no idea what he just did?

"Look, never mind," I said, helping him up. "What are you doing over on this side of town, then? Do you remember that, at least?"

"Trying to find Nige. That bastard owes me brass from the other night. I thought he worked today."

"Nige doesn't work here!"

Gangrene looked around, inspecting Fresh Slab. "You sure?"

I stared at him. "Yes."

His forehead wrinkled, and then he shrugged. "He did look a little different today..."

"That's Paul, you nit!" I shook my head, my eyes rolling skyward. "And where's the rest of my cleanser?"

He patted me on the shoulder. "Sorry, mate. Had to use it all to get the job done."

"Damn it, Green! Why couldn't you have gone to the shops for it, then? Mr. White busts me for this kind of shit!"

Gangrene started feeling around his pockets. "Here, mate. Have some of this instead." He stuffed something into my trouser pocket and trudged off towards the door. Not even turning his head, he raised a hand and waved.

Behind me, a customer called out for a sale. I easily talked the guy into buying two more singles, discovering only after he left that Bugs had set Gangrene's weapon on the counter.

The gun had to go. I didn't know where I was going to put it, but I had to get it out of there.

And what of Gangrene's 'payment'? I slipped my fingers into my pocket and pulled out a wad of crumpled fivers. The bastard was worried about getting money from Nige, but here he was handing me twenty-five quid!

I made a mental note in case Edwards caught up with me, then started hunting for a good hiding place.

Fingerprints. If Gangrene used up all the bullets before he got to Beaufort Market, and I'd been holding the gun after I knocked him out, then the blame would be on me. Reaching under the counter, I took out one of Mr. White's hankies. A dab of glass cleaner and some thorough wiping would remove all traces of my touch. I rubbed until the cool metal gleamed and my reflection was visible. Then I wrapped the gun in the handkerchief, being careful not to touch the surface again with my fingers. The perfect hiding place came to mind: a crevice beneath one of the record shelves. I remember running out of wood and having to stick the shelf near the back of the stall to hide the gaping mistake.

The hole was about as large as an open palm and now filled with cobwebs. I was on my hands and knees in order to reach the spot, praying a customer wouldn't enter and find me in such a suspicious position.

I shoved the shrouded gun into the hole as far as I could, coughing on a cloud of dust created by my movement. When the gun hit the base of the next shelf, I was satisfied.

Business was slow the rest of the afternoon, and the place was strangely silent. Usually Poly in the stall near ours had a nice crowd of mates hanging about, but today she wasn't there. The stand across from Fresh Slab closed early so that its owner could spend the evening with Paul. And upstairs, I heard no thumping of feet or creaking of floorboards. Beaufort Market was deserted.

I sat back against the dusty wall, still looking at the place where I hid Gangrene's gun, but my eyes were concentrating on the darkness inside. It wasn't a matter of heroin overdosing now. It couldn't be. I knew Susan enough to know that she wouldn't do any of that shit. The only way would be by force. And would Gangrene do that? He was absolutely insane today, so I couldn't tell. But what I could tell was that it wasn't a dealer I had to bust; it was a murderer.

"*Jon?*"

A voice startled me out of my thoughts, making me crack my skull against the wall.

"I'm down here," I groaned, holding my hand to my head.

"What happened?" Mary asked. "Are you all right?"

"Yeah," I replied. "I was just thinking." I felt a lump starting on the back of my head.

Mary chuckled when she saw that I was okay. "Maybe you should leave the thinking to Caoilinn, luv." She held out a hand and helped me up off the floor.

I stuck my tongue out at her teasingly.

"Do you think you'll be recovered enough to help me with the zine tonight?"

"I'll have to ring Aunt Vi to see if she'll let us borrow her typewriter first."

Mary closed up the shop while I begged my aunt to let us stop there on the way back to my flat. She eventually agreed under the condition that we didn't "make a scene," which basically meant we'd have to stealthily slip ourselves into her house so that none of her neighbors would ask her about us the next day.

$$\neq$$

"Did you see that?"

I had just finished locking the doors to Beaufort Market when Mary grabbed my arm tightly.

"Over there," she whispered, pointing towards a building on King's Road.

The sky was beginning to darken outside, but the streetlights hadn't turned on yet. My eyes were trying to adjust, and I squinted to see if something looked different. The spaces between the tall storefronts were pitch black. I focused on the spot Mary motioned towards, but couldn't see anything unusual.

"What was it, Maire?"

"Someone was there. It looked like the same bloke who's been following me for the past few days."

I turned to her quickly. *"What?!"*

Mary nodded, her eyes still fixed on the dark building. "I saw him at the pub as I was cleaning up a few days ago, but couldn't make out his face or anything."

"Why didn't you tell me about this before?" I asked her excitedly.

"Well, I didn't think much of it at the time," Mary retorted. "I mean, why should I have?"

My nerves were reeling. Were we next on the hit list?

"But then I started seeing him everywhere I went. Always like a hundred yards away, but the same bloke. Tall, thin, in a Macintosh... a trench coat."

Just then Mary shot her hand out again. "*There!* He's there!"

I caught him in the corner of my eye before he slid back into the shadows. Adrenaline began to kick in, and I lurched forward, running towards him.

"Jon, no!" Mary yelled after me.

I could hear the scuffling of shoes against the pavement, and I pulled out my switchblade. But by the time I got to where we saw him, he was gone.

Mary ran to me as I stood there panting.

"Come on, let's get out of here before something really does happen," she said nervously, tugging me towards Sloane Square. She hugged the storefronts as we walked, and I held tight to her. But my head was turned, and I had that building behind us in the corner of my eye. I saw nothing—no rustling, no stretching of shadows; he had become one with the darkness. We walked briskly, silently, our ears searching for any sounds not coming from our feet. When a passing cab slowed, we waved for a ride.

Aunt Violet owned a Georgian terrace in Hampstead. The neighborhood she lived in was fairly conservative (though not nearly as conservative as she'd have me believe), and using this as an excuse, Aunt Vi discouraged any daytime visits. *"Truly, you must understand, Jonathan. What would the neighbors say if they were to see you at my door? Why, they would dial 999, most certainly!"* she'd remind me when I was safely in her foyer.

As the cab drove down her street, I saw that Aunt Vi's house was the only one with its outside lamps off. It wasn't even necessary to know her address—her house was always the one not beckoning a visit.

I paid the driver quickly and watched him speed away. Aunt Vi peeked out of her window, then cracked the door open just enough for us to squeeze through. She ushered us frantically into her sitting room.

"A cup of tea then, dear?" Aunt Vi asked Mary.

Mary accepted politely. I'd noticed that Aunt Vi took to Mary more than any of my other friends, and I tried to use that to my advantage whenever possible. This night was no exception. Aunt Vi had agreed to let me borrow her typewriter not because I asked nicely (which I did) but because I had told her that Mary needed to use it to type out a university paper. Mary scolded me about the story earlier: *"How are you going to explain it to her when she finds out that I'm not even _at_ university?"* But Aunt Vi wouldn't know. I was sure that she made up her own stories as well, for the sake of conversation. It was a wonder she could even keep half of them straight.

"Now, see, Jonathan—if you were to go to university like your friend here, you could be doing much more productive things than spending time at the police station." Aunt Vi was perched on the chair across from us, delicately sipping her tea.

I felt a little kick from Mary.

Aunt Vi shook her head softly. "I almost dare not show my face at the Ladies' Club luncheons."

"Really, Aunt Vi, Bugs and I didn't do anything wrong," I sighed. "And how would anyone there know, anyway?"

Mary smoothed out her skirt, hiding a small snag in the material.

Aunt Vi took another calm sip of her tea and replied: "Well, surely they would hear it from the Chief Inspector. He only lives a few houses away, after all."

To that I said nothing; I merely swallowed a rising cough and stifled the paranoia out of my head. *Don't turn into Tony*, I begged myself. *Now's not the time for conspiracy theories.* Mary fidgeted next to me, perhaps looking for a different topic to steer the conversation.

"And, really, Jonathan...he's only worried for your well-being. It would do you good to listen to him."

Aunt Vi poured Mary some more tea and continued: "I do wish you'd settle yourself a bit. I'm sure you and your friends have gotten that man's nerves tied. You know it's only been a few months since he lost his daughter. And so young she was..." Aunt Vi shook her head again and sat back down, holding her cup daintily.

I put my tea down. All I wanted was the bleeding typewriter, not another sob story. This week had already brought enough melodrama that a sad Chief Inspector was the least of my worries. But it hit me, as she continued talking about his daughter's illness, that with Edwards as her neighbor, Aunt Vi's house was no longer a safe haven. If what she said was true, he'd probably be checking up on me all the time, knowing that she was my legal link to London.

"...and Miriam said he was being very brave, since she saw him just before the funeral and he was weeping in the church. Can you just imagine? The poor dear. I made him some puddings, which he liked very much. I'd give you the recipe, but I really don't think you would be able to make them without my assistance. You probably don't even have the correct pans, do you? Mary, darling, you really should help get him in order. Why, Miriam suggested..."

"Aunt Vi, I think we ought to get going. Mary needs time to work on her paper."

Mary kicked me again, but this time not so hard. She smiled graciously at my aunt. "I really appreciate you letting me borrow your typewriter,

Mrs. Broster. I promise I'll have it back to you as soon as possible."

"No, no, you take your time, dear," Aunt Vi said with a quick wave of her hand.

≠

Back at my flat, we used our resources wisely. It seemed all of the utilities were up-and-running, so we took advantage of them and worked through the night. Our first issue of *Scabbed Over* would be the start of our attempt at putting together a puzzle—one I knew we were already a significant piece of.

Mary sat at the typewriter, her fingers clicking out an article. I thought the cover should be cut-and-paste (like a ransom note), so I was crunched up on the floor cutting out newsprint letters from the day's *Guardian* and scattering them out for us to pick from.

"We should put a request in here for anyone who knows anything about what's been happening lately to contact us," Mary suggested.

"Don't you think we should have our issues be anonymous, though? I mean, considering the circumstances?"

Mary stopped typing and was silent for a moment.

"I hadn't thought about that," she finally said.

"Well, maybe we can write persuasive-enough articles that people will start talking. And then we can hear it on the streets, at the pubs and shows," I offered.

Mary turned around and smiled. "You know, sometimes you can be so clever, Jonathan Alton Hunter," she teased in a mock-Aunt Vi accent. "You just simply must apply yourself."

I held up the temporary cover I made for her approval.

Apply, I will, I thought. *Just you wait and see.*

SIX

Is Boise Lou At It Again?

The title screamed off the page, and I felt my grin widening.

"Looks good, doesn't it?" Mary asked proudly. She had just stopped in at Fresh Slab with a stack of newly-printed copies of the first issue of our zine. "And look what I found."

Mary dragged in a small metal newspaper stand. It stood about three feet high and was fairly rusty.

"Where'd you get that?"

"I nicked it from one of the shops down the way," she winked.

I laughed as she slipped off to McSurley's. The little stand was perfect for *Scabbed Over*, so I placed the copies on it and admired our work until customers arrived. It was an impressive first issue, as first issues go. We had it printed on A4 paper that was sliced in half then stapled once in the corner. I handwrote out an article on the upcoming Queen's Jubilee as well as all the concert and record reviews. Mary composed the pages-long first installment of our crime-solving attempt and typed it up cleanly, which was laudable since I couldn't figure out how to put the ribbon in without getting inky fingerprints all over the place.

We made 50p on the zines by day's end, which, considering we'd never done this before, wasn't too bad. Our sales were helped by the fact that I spent the day reading a copy while I sat by the counter, wanting to absorb every nuance of our creation. Mary had suggested that we set out a 'clue box' where our readers could slip in any clues of their own in response to the article Mary penned. I tried to make it look like I had nothing to do with the publication—that I was just selling it—so I lied when customers asked anything about its origin. Maybe the idea of a good mystery was all someone needed to give us the answers necessary to solve this whole mess.

Paul had been telling me about a bloke who was hanging around the old apartment at King's Cross yesterday, and it sounded like a real lead. If I could link it to the guy who was following Mary, maybe we could move closer to the end of this horror show. I started compiling a list of potential suspects that I could go over with Paul, but he hadn't shown up yet. Then the realization hit me that he'd certainly had a good time with the gal in the shop across the way, and I knew I'd just

catch up with him tonight after Mary and I returned from
Crawley.

In the breaks between customers, I scribbled my suspicions on the back of an old envelope. I knew I wasn't the culprit, and I couldn't see why Mary or Paul would be involved, so I eliminated us from the pool. Boise Lou and the Teds topped off my list, since they seemed most likely to strike out at us. The victims were all within the punk circle, so it logically followed that they'd be involved. But then Gangrene would be involved, too; drug overdoses were in his line of work. And he really didn't get along with Susan, so maybe he wanted her out of the picture. I couldn't just discard that idea, even though it felt like a far stretch. I thought about Tony, but shook my head. He was paranoid, but he really was getting somewhere with Susan. What motivation would he have to kill her? And Julie? It didn't fit. Same with Bugs. Sure, he had violent mood swings, but I couldn't find a motive for why he'd want any of the girls dead. And what of Tony's mumblings about Nige? Nige had links to each of the girls and he certainly got around. Hell, he was with two of them just hours before they died. I wrote his name down on my list. Tony had his connections, and if he thought Nige might be responsible, I wouldn't immediately discount it. I also wouldn't totally discount his thoughts that the police were in on it somehow, so I wrote down Edwards and Jeffreys. They were always on our backs; the opportunity was definitely there. And Jeffreys seemed to be out to get us in any way he could. Still, I admit I felt kind of silly thinking they'd bother going through such trouble for no particularly good reason, so I put a question mark next to each of their names to make it look as though I weren't so stupid.

So, with my list in hand, where would I start? I thought Mary's article was the best place. We'd go to the top first—to the Teds. But who could be our go-between? I peeked my head out of Fresh Slab to see if Paul's date had opened up her shop yet this morning. Her stall was dark. If she had been there, I might have gathered up the courage to ask her to listen in on some Teddy Boy gossip. She had quite a few Teds for customers and would know more than me about what was going on in their circle.

I stewed over all of this for the afternoon. What were the motives for these crimes? Is it possible that the deaths weren't even related? Was I reading more into these unfortunate events than I should? Maybe hanging around Tony was clouding my rational mind.

Crime scenes told stories—why didn't I pay more attention when I was at them? I scrounged through the shelves under the till and found a couple small plastic bags. In the movies, detectives put clues in little bags; perhaps I'd pay a visit to Susan's crime scene and see if I could find anything the police might have missed. It certainly couldn't hurt.

Mary stopped in as the sun began to set, having left work early so we could meet a couple of her friends at The Rocket. I wasn't really in the mood to head to Crawley, but I gave in because behind her glittering eyes I knew she was scared to go alone. Plus, maybe we could find out something else about Tommy's death that would help us explain these new ones.

"Any clues in the box?" she asked, her voice perky with anticipation.

"Maire, we just put the issues out this morning!"

She wrinkled her lips. "Well, I thought they'd be talking already!"

I chuckled to myself. Mary hummed along to the awful Eater single I had jokingly stuck on the record player. She started shuffling the record stacks so that everything looked clean and even, her body wiggling a little to the music while her hands worked. Her hair was tousled from running the pub, dyed-black strands begging to be smoothed down in place, light hitting the tips so that they looked blue, like a comic book hairdo. Mary was dressed in one of my worn t-shirts, the little vinyl mini-skirt that I bought for her last year when I found 20 quid on the tube, and fishnet stockings that turned her white legs grey. With my eyes I followed the length of each one slowly, memorizing the curves of her calves, inching my way up her thighs. My body warmed at the thought of her draped across something in my apartment, wearing little more than a crown of barbed wire, snarling at me from the corner, growling *"I'll take what I want of you, however I want to, whenever I want to..."* Then, on all fours above me, licking my lips, panting, biting at my neck, until I can't bear it anymore...

"Jon!"

I blinked.

Mary was standing in front of me, hands on her hips.

"I swear, I've never met anyone who stares off into space more than you do! Did you even hear a sodding word I said?"

I nodded, but she just shook her head, smirking.

"I cleaned everything up, so let's go. I want to catch the girls before the place gets too loud."

We locked up and headed out, but on our way to the tube station I pulled Mary aside and asked her to give me a few minutes at the spot where Susan was attacked. Plastic bags in hand, we crouched down and scoured the ground, finding the usual alley trash: cigarette butts, broken pint bottles, crumbled mortar. But out of the corner of my eye, I saw something shimmer. The fading sun glinted off of Mary's necklace, which, in turn, struck a couple faint rays of light on the concrete beneath us.

"Maire, look at this," I said as I reached out carefully, using the filter end of a spent cigarette to move the object closer to me. It was a needle that looked to be broken off of a syringe.

"How could they have missed that?" Mary questioned. She inspected the thin piece of metal as I carefully placed it into my bag.

"Well, it was against the foundation over here, and it really was dark out. Maybe it didn't mean anything to them? I mean, they're the detectives; they should know what a good clue is." I didn't believe myself as I spoke, but I couldn't come up with a better answer.

Mary stared at the ground beside me. "Here's something, too."

She put the bag over her fingers and picked up a piece of mangled plastic.

"It looks like a dog got to it," she said, holding it up to try to see it better before the sun disappeared. "I think it was a biro."

I wanted to check it out, but Mary slipped her hand out of the bag and shoved the wadded-up clue into my pocket. Behind us in the street we could hear Teds heckling someone, and it seemed like a pretty good time to get out of there.

Crawley was a decent train ride south of central London, a little ways past Gatwick airport. I didn't like leaving the big city for the bland suburban life, but Mary's friends Rachel and Michelle lived there so I couldn't protest too

much. Especially not now, as they had been friends of
Tommy, a possible link to what was now going on in our own circle of friends here in London.

It was Mary's idea to meet Rachel and Michelle somewhere casual, so it was planned that we'd all head to The Rocket, a proper-looking Crawley pub. The facade was cleanly-painted in white with a standard yellow frieze strip along the top proclaiming in white letters that the place was, in fact, known as The Rocket.

But such a traditional exterior betrayed the noise that filled the smoky interior as we entered. Mary had promised me that her friends would be easy to find and that the night would be short, but what we were welcomed into would assure us that any plans to leave within the hour were foiled. Despite how awful the band sounded, with a loud guitar over total feedback distortion, the pub was warmly packed with people.

This must be what punk sounds like to people who aren't from London, I thought, chuckling a bit to myself.

As Mary searched for Rachel and Michelle in the crowd, I stayed at the bar, hoping to get as drunk as all the people around me. The man standing to my left raved about how the band was going to be the next Buzzcocks, but the bartender chimed in that these guys hadn't even been booked tonight.

"They're only up there because the band that was scheduled had to cancel," he quipped. "Sorry blokes, the lot of them."

The bartender shook his head pathetically, and I watched the band for a while. After a few pints they were seeming pretty decent. They tried hard at what they were doing, but the sound just wasn't working right. You couldn't hear a damn thing but that awful guitar!

Between songs I watched for Mary. About a half hour into the set I saw that she was chatting with a girl, but my eyes had begun to blur a bit so I couldn't tell if it was Rachel or Michelle or just some tart she ran into.

I tried to focus on them, staring intently as though, miraculously, my clear vision would return. But just as I reached the height of my effort, the guy who was still next to me slumped over onto my shoulder.

"They're brilliant, mate, don't you think?" he blubbered, waving a drunken hand toward the band. "Bloody Buzzcocks, mate..."

Someone on his other side shoved him once, in turn knocking my current pint onto the bar counter.

"It's the Easy Cure, you bastard, not the Buzzcocks! We're not in London!" the bloke scolded.

"Rachel told me something interesting," Mary shouted over the noise when she finally returned to me.

I tried to ask her what it was, but non-words slipped out from my numb lips.

"How many pints have you had?" she asked, grabbing hold of my shoulder.

I shrugged. The drinks had taken their full toll. Next to me, the drunk Buzzcocks guy snored against the counter and no one bothered to wake him. I felt like doing the same thing, and Mary must have noticed by the way I was swaying. She tugged me towards the door, and that was the last I remembered.

In the morning I found Mary's clothes on the floor next to my bed as I looked for a quick place to be sick. My stomach churned, made worse by the smell of Mary frying something for breakfast. Luckily, I managed to crawl to the toilet in time. I couldn't remember how many drinks I had, or even *what* I had. I just remembered being in fucking Crawley.

When I cleaned myself up a bit, I trudged out to the kitchen. Mary was at the stove trying to keep the burner lit. She had on my ratty t-shirt from yesterday and apparently nothing else as I could see the soft white curves of her bum peeking out from beneath the ragged hem. If I hadn't felt so sick I would have shagged her against the refrigerator right then and there, but my head pounded and I had to sit down before my legs gave way.

"The refrigerator's not working this morning," Mary said once she saw me at the table. "I figured I'd better salvage anything I could." She put a plate of freshly-fried bacon and eggs in front of me. "It's a good thing you never keep too much in there."

I reached for a cigarette. The only thing I could hold down that morning was a lungful of nicotine.

Mary understood and helped herself to my plate, nibbling away as though it were the first hot meal she'd had in a long time. She picked at the fat on the bacon, discarding the rubbery part that hadn't crisped all the way. Then she licked the salty grease off her fingertips. Her fork moved the eggs around the plate, but never met her lips. When she realized I was observing her, she winked and blew kisses at me.

"Are you feeling any better?" she asked.

I nodded. The nausea was slowly starting to subside.

We chatted a bit as I helped her wash up. It was Saturday, and Mary only worked at the pub on weekdays, so if she didn't have plans she would usually spend the weekend at Fresh Slab. That was a big help to Paul and me as the weekends were our busiest times, and Mr. White refused to hire any additional clerks.

Mary had grown quiet by the time we got to the shop. I knew she was thinking about Susan again. All I could do was squeeze her hand. She responded likewise, and we left it at that.

Beaufort Market was bustling with activity when we entered, but Fresh Slab was dark and closed-up.

"That's odd. Isn't Paul usually the first one here?" Mary asked quizzically.

I looked over and saw that Carol, the woman who owned the clothing stand across the way, was already busy with customers, so there was no chance that he was with her having a lie-in.

"Maybe he's just running late. You know that if he doesn't get to the tube station by nine he has to wait for a totally different connection," I offered. Still, with everything that had been happening lately, I felt a slight tinge of nervousness prickle through me.

I unlocked the gates around the stall and pushed them back out of the way. Mary flicked the light switch on and started arranging some of the displays. A mod came up asking if we had the new Jam record and Mary told him to piss off, which helped lighten the mood a bit.

"So, did you ever get to see Rachel and Michelle last night?" I asked Mary between customers.

"Well, only Rachel showed up, but I didn't get to tell you what I found out..." She rolled her eyes at me as if to say (in a particularly snippy Irish accent) *"...because you were banjaxed."*

I frowned and motioned for her to continue while I was still willing to listen.

"First off, she said the police never officially

declared Tommy's death an overdose or a homicide because they're still trying to determine what he died from first—drugs or internal bleeding."

I squinted involuntarily. Something dodgy was definitely going on—if they couldn't determine which killed him, then what exactly led up to his death? Was he sitting there in the station shooting up a minute before he got the shit beaten out of him? How could he have done it after he was assaulted as badly as he was? An image of Susan battered in the alley flashed before my eyes. Did someone forcibly inject him? And if so, why?

Mary continued: "Rachel also told me that they said it was heroin, but... I don't know, a purer form or something. What they found during the autopsy was different than what they were used to seeing."

Maybe that's why they got the Chief Inspector involved, I thought.

"But that's not all. She said that the last time she talked to him was a couple days before he died, and he had just been up here having a huge fight with Nige over some bint."

My eyes widened. "Did she say which girl?" I hoped it was one of the victims, at least to narrow down my suspects.

Mary shook her head. "She couldn't remember. It was someone she never heard him talk about before."

I frowned. "Well, that's not much of a clue then."

A couple hours flew by with a steady stream of customers, and I sold out of all the Stranglers stuff we had on display. It was crazy for a while, with more people in that little space than should be physically possible. We even had more takers on our zine, which was hopeful.

Mary tried to think of a new use for Paul's now-empty display while I sat at the counter pouring over my list of suspects. I wanted to believe that I narrowed it down to the right people, but what if it was someone I didn't even know? I glanced over at our clue box and was shocked to see two pieces of paper—one folded and one crumpled—stuffed into it.

But before I could reach over and pick them out, my attention was caught by a squeal from Mary. My eyes darted over to her and found that she was rubbing her bum. Suddenly, she shot out the hardest slap I've ever seen to Boise Lou, who was standing in the entryway.

"Sorry, doll, I didn't see you there," he snickered at her while feeling his stinging face.

"What the bloody hell is going on?" I growled, rising from my seat and reaching behind me for my switchblade.

Boise held his hand up. "Settle down there, Hunter." He smiled, and I noticed one of his teeth had a gold cap to it.

"Yeah, we didn't come here for you," Brody quipped from behind him. He spoke with a heavy Scottish brogue.

No wonder he doesn't talk much.

Boise turned his head, snapping his fingers

once, and Brody was silenced.

I kept Mary in the corner of my eye. She had moved from the display and looked as though she were ready to take Brody on if he tried to lunge for me. And I was bracing myself. If she held off Brody long enough (and I was sure she could), I'd be able to take Boise on my own.

"We're looking for your little rasta friend," Boise finally said.

"Yeah, well, he's not here," I spat out, "so why don't you just piss off..."

Boise smiled and shook his head slightly. "He ought to watch himself."

I stiffened.

"I take my crew very seriously, Hunter." Boise leaned in to me. "And if I find out that little bastard breaks Carol's heart, he's going to be very sorry he didn't stick to his own kind."

I reacted by moving my hand out to shove him, but he caught it in mid-air and held it between us.

Mary saw what was happening and kicked Brody in the shin. He crunched over, howling. She reached down, grabbing his hair, and cracked his head against her knee. God, I loved that girl.

Boise let go of me and smacked Brody away while Mary stood seething. Brody moaned, and Boise tugged him out of our stall.

"Don't test me, Hunter," Boise said as he left Beaufort Market, the sound of his voice bouncing off the ceiling. "I know just where to find you."

I hadn't realized my jaw was clenched until Mary came over to my side.

"Stupid cunt," she said, rubbing my back. "He better watch that *I'm* not around. I'll.. I'll..." She let out a little snarl, but didn't finish her sentence. We were both still staring at the door, expecting him to return.

Finally, I exhaled my held breath and sat back down. Surely, there had to be a more cushy retail job than this.

"Jon, we've got clues!" Mary exclaimed when she glanced past me at the box.

"Open them up and read them to me," I said, flipping an old receipt pad over to take notes on. As she took the papers out of the box, I scribbled down what just happened with Boise, feeling sure I'd need it for future reference.

Mary carefully opened up the wadded one and read: "*Boise won't help you. It's Dan you have to watch.*"

I jotted that down, not sure if it was a trick by a Ted (based on what I just saw) or a real clue.

Then Mary unfolded the other note and said curiously: "*Don't you see—it all started with Stacie.*"

We both looked at each other with questioning eyes. "Who's Stacie?"

Mary slipped the notes into her jacket pocket. "I could just be getting paranoid, but I swear I saw that bloke again last night."

"Are you serious?" I asked, wishing I hadn't been so drunk at the pub.

Mary nodded. "That's why I made you leave so soon. I didn't know what else to do."

"Did you get a good look at him this time?"

"Well, all I can tell is that he's tall, lean, and white. And definitely a bloke. Oh, and something on him kept sparkling, like a piercing or a filling."

So, that appeared to count out Gangrene and Jeffreys, both of whom were only about my height, 5'8". It could, however, confirm the other three suspects left on my list: Boise, Nige, and Edwards. Still, Gangrene knew all the tricks of the trade when it came to drugs, and Jeffreys really seemed to have it out for us. Not to mention the fact that one of those clues Mary and I found at Susan's crime scene was a mangled pen—the same kind even that I saw Jeffreys chewing on.

Or maybe the bloke was someone we never even met before? He could be a hit-man, out to get us because we already knew too much...

"Hello, James Bond, are you there?"

Mary was staring at me.

"I said, maybe we should check up on Paul."

"Oh, yeah, right." I blinked myself out of my thoughts.

Mary grabbed some pence and went to the phone box outside. I helped a couple customers and started tidying up a bit. The receipts were a mess, and I wished Paul would arrive already since he was better at sorting that stuff out than me.

A few minutes later, Mary returned.

"I let the phone ring and ring and ring, but he didn't pick up. I'm going to talk to Carol."

As I was filing records, I watched her pull Carol to the side and chat. Carol didn't look too pleased with the conversation, and I started to wonder if the date hadn't gone as planned. Paul didn't phone me either way, so I had just assumed everything was fine.

Mary ran back to me, leaving Carol standing there by her stall, watching.

"Jon, I'm worried now."

"What did she say?"

"She thought they had a great time the other night, but he never rang her back yesterday, and each time she tried to reach him, there was no answer. She even went by his place and nothing. Do you think he would have stood her up like that?"

Carol slowly walked back into her shop with a customer.

"Something's not right, Maire." I started to shiver. "Come on, we need to find him."

SEVEN

"Knock harder!" I yelled to Mary from the side of Paul's building. I had wedged myself between the fire escape and a thick vine in the hope that I would be able to peer into a window to see what Paul was up to. Yet, at the same time, I feared finding a body on the floor or blood on the walls. My imagination became more vivid as the moments passed. What if he was slumped in the bath with two days' rot set in? Or scattered across the kitchen in gory bits?

"Can you see anything?" Mary called out, her voice starting to sound fearful.

I could hear her tugging at the door handle, jiggling it at first, then banging her side against the heavy wood in an attempt to break in.

"Not really; I need to get in closer."

I assessed the strength of the old vine with my boot. It appeared to cling to the brick wall tightly. If I could keep one foot on the fire escape and pull myself up a bit to the concrete ledge, I'd have a clear view into his living room area, which peeked into the bedroom and bathroom at an angle. That way, I'd kill three birds with one stone, so to speak. Or myself, if I wasn't careful about it; there'd be a decent fall down as Paul's flat was on the third floor.

Mary began to pick the lock, and she tried to force the handle some more. It was a relief that Paul's flat faced an alley, since, with all the noise we were making, someone would have surely caught sight of us and called the police by now.

I moved slowly and cautiously, my hands gripping the ledge above me. With my right foot I got a little boost off the fire escape and pulled myself up. In a few blinks I glanced into the flat: nothing looked ransacked, no lights had been left on, and there was no Paul.

But as I began to ease myself back down, I thought I caught a pair of eyes in the darkness. I struck out at the window instinctively, but while doing so, I lost my footing. Desperately, I clawed at the ledge, kicking my feet a little too wildly in an attempt to reconnect with the vine. There was a loud crack, and a huge chunk of dried vine fell to the ground below. With nothing for my feet to latch onto, I gripped the concrete as tightly as possible. I felt my arms shake, not used to needing this much strength. And then my hands started to sweat and sting, the pain returning from when I cut them on my broken cup. My fingers tired and slipped on the crumbly cement.

"*Maire!*" I yelped, but it was already too late. I caught sight of her panicked face as I fell.

Mary's frantic footsteps down the fire escape echoed through the alley. "*Jon!*" she cried, running as quickly as she could towards me.

Thankfully, a pile of black-bagged rubbish broke my fall. It could have been a hell of a lot worse than it looked, otherwise. I involuntarily let out a groan as Mary tried to help me up. My hip ached like it was hit by the wing of a car. I prayed that nothing was broken, but I couldn't tell yet because my body was still tingling from the adrenaline rush.

"Are you okay?" Her eyes were wide and trembled in their sockets.

I nodded as I picked gravel out of the scrapes on my palms. "I thought I saw someone move in the shadows."

"Paul?"

Shaking my head, I replied: "Nothing was there. Not Paul, not a mess, nothing. My reflection in the dirty glass, maybe."

$$\neq$$

Mary grabbed the phone and began the rounds as I cleaned myself up. I inspected the damage done under the falling water, which had already grown cold. My hip was definitely bruised, moreso than I originally thought. I also noticed a gash on my shoulder that I hadn't felt before. The soap stung at the wound and on my scraped hands. I was a right mess.

"Bugs and Tony haven't seen him," Mary said as I limped out to her. "And I tried everyone else I could think of. I'm going downstairs for the telephone directory to try the hospitals."

"Yeah, well, I'm going with you." I wasn't about to let her out of my sight with that stalker running around loose out there.

She gave me a look asking if I was sure I could make it, but she saw I was serious when I started down the hall.

"You read off the numbers, I'll dial," Mary said as we stood in a phone box outside my apartment building. We were prepared to go through the whole alphabet if we had to, intent on calling each hospital listed in London. I tore the page out of the directory and began at the top. The answers we had been getting were the same: that they hadn't admitted anyone by that name. But when we hit the "saint" listings, the answer changed.

"She's transferring me!" Mary gasped.

I didn't know whether to be relieved or panicked, so I just stood there shivering.

"Yes, thank you, I'm trying to locate a Paul Scrivener."

Mary gripped the receiver tightly to stop her hands from shaking. Then she bit her lip. "No, but we're his friends. I don't think he has much family here." The corners of her eyes started to glisten.

I tried to listen to the woman on the other end, but the sound of the street around us blurred her words.

"Can we see him, at least?" she asked softly.

There was a long pause before Mary continued: "Yes, yes, thank you. We will."

My hands reached for her gently.

Mary hung up the phone and began to cry. "He's at St. Stephen's."

"Well, what happened? Is he okay?"

She shook her head, hands at her eyes, and was too choked up to tell me.

I pulled her out to the street with me and felt in my pocket to be sure I had enough money. As soon as a cab headed our way, I waved it down.

≠

I gripped Paul's hand tightly in mine, biting my lip til it bled in an effort to contain the anger and tears that screamed to be expelled. He laid there hooked up to machines that breathed for him. Every so often I'd think that I felt a twitch of one of his fingers, and I'd get hopeful that his swollen eyes would open...but, nothing.

The doctor was talking with Mary, who had been able to collect herself by that time. He hadn't thought that Paul would make it past the first night, so every moment, coma or not, was a miracle.

Paul was beaten almost beyond recognition. It was as though someone had taken a bat to him and didn't know when to stop. The brown skin of his face looked black from the bruises and distorted by the swelling. Heavy bandages covered most of the rest of his body, save the hand I held. Enough bones had been fractured that even if he hadn't been in a coma, he'd still have to remain in the hospital for an indeterminate amount of time.

"Hang in there, man," I whispered to him. "I promise you, I'll find this bastard. You just keep your end of the deal and be around when I get the job done."

"Until he regains consciousness, there's not much else I can tell you other than whatever happened out there, your friend put up a good fight. Many of the injuries he sustained are consistent with defensive wounds."

Mary sniffed and I looked down.

"I've set the bones and stitched the cuts, so it's a matter of time until he heals from them. All we can do is monitor his progress and hope that he comes around soon." The doctor reached over and patted my back.

I felt my eyes glisten, then inhaled deeply to fight it back. "Thanks... for not giving up."

"I noticed something odd, though," the doctor continued.

Mary moved to my side.

"Although I found no trace of any foreign substances in his blood and no indication he was an habitual drug user, I did notice a few fresh puncture marks on his chest and arm."

"You mean, like from a needle?" Mary asked.

The doctor nodded. "If something in a syringe had been injected in one of the places on his chest where I found the marks, he'd have surely died there on the street."

My stomach flipped a few times, and the nausea I felt that morning returned. Mary wrapped her arms around me and rested her face against my chest. It was only a matter of time before this person got to us, too, and I was sure we were next. I needed to find the guy that had been following Mary, as he was now the most important clue.

We hid ourselves away in my flat the following day. It was time to come up with a plan. Somehow, we had to find a way to grab that mystery guy.

"You know, Jon, the quickest way is to use me as bait," Mary quipped between all my complex suggestions. "I mean, it's pretty obvious he wants me next." She stood in front of the bathroom mirror with an ice cube behind her ear, trying to add a new piercing to her collection.

"No way," I retorted. "That's too risky." I leaned against the door frame to keep the weight off my bruised hip.

Mary's lips curled. "Do you want me to play in his game, or him to play in ours? Because that's what it's going to come down to." She cringed as the pin went through, then dumped rubbing alcohol on her ear lobe.

I shook my head. "No, there's got to be another way."

"Jon, we have to be ready for him. We need to be in control of the encounter. Otherwise it's just dumb luck if we grab him. And that's the chance we can't afford to take."

"You know Keely would never forgive me if something happened to you."

She frowned for a second, then regained her stance just as quickly. "Caoilinn has her own hands full at the moment."

"Okay, here's an idea," Mary said later from the floor.

I rolled over a bit on the couch so I could see her.

"Most of the people on our list of suspects will be at The Rainbow tomorrow night, right?"

The Clash was bringing their 'White Riot' tour to the old theatre, which (even though Mary didn't really like them all that much) we knew we'd go to because it was a pretty big deal.

"Yeah—I'm sure we'll see Gangrene and Nige," I said. "And Boise will probably find his way there just to fuck with someone."

"Well, maybe not...I mean, that area is too black for Teds to just be roaming around."

Mary had a point; it wasn't really an area Teds happened to frequent.

"We can always drop in at your Aunt's place if we want to check out Edwards," she continued. "And Jeffreys...well, I'm sure it's not too hard to find him."

"He seems to find Bugs easily enough."

Mary tickled my chin with her toes. "So, who do you want to take?"

I grabbed her ankle and gave it a little tug. "You."She giggled and squirmed on the floor, retracting her leg from my grip. "At the show, silly."

I reached back down and stroked her cheek. "I'll go for Boise and the cops if they show up. And I'll also keep my eye on Gangrene. You take Nige."

The plan we settled on was this: I would get Bugs as back-up while Mary would have Tony. Then she and I would split up and monitor any suspicious activity on the part of our suspects. If we saw a situation that looked like a precursor to another crime, we'd intervene. I suggested starting a fight to cause a distraction, if necessary. Anything that could buy us time until the police arrived. Or until I could figure out who the real culprit was; whichever came first. We'd

also check in with each other at the end of each band's
set in case we garnered information that would require us to change our game-plan.

It was the best thing we could come up with. A quick call to Bugs confirmed that our plan would be executed upon arrival.

≠

"Jon, are you awake?" Mary whispered to me in the darkness of the bedroom.

I squeezed her close in response.

"I can't sleep."

"Me neither," I replied.

Mary sighed and pressed her face against me. I ran my fingers through her hair carefully, counting each strand. The image of Miranda's tousled locks splayed out on the bathroom tile shot through my mind. The thought of Julie frozen on the floor, the memory of Susan fading in the alley, the battered body of Paul laying comatose in a hospital...

"Do you think we'll ever find him?" Mary asked softly.

I blinked away the rising anger inside and cleared my throat a bit. "Yes. I just hope we don't find him too late."

≠

When I got to Fresh Slab in the morning, I found Mr. White behind the counter. The shop wasn't completely open for business yet as he hadn't pulled the gate around to the side or set out any displays. He had receipts spread across the tabletop and was hurriedly looking for something.

"I know, I know; I heard about Paul from Carol," Mr. White said as I entered, not even looking up at me. He started pulling things from underneath the counter. "Did you use all the cleanser already?" he asked.

"Well, we had an accident the other day..." I lied, hoping he'd spare me the lecture.

"*Damn* it!" he cursed from the floor. His fist slammed against the counter.

I took a step back. "I'm sorry, Mr. White. I... I'll go down to the shops and buy more."

Mr. White stood up slowly, gripping the wood. "No, that's not important." He grumbled and shook his head. "Marla's taking me for all I'm worth. She found out about Stacie and now she wants half of the businesses and every sodding thing I own."

Stacie?

"She wants a divorce?"

"Oh, I'll give her that, all right," he growled. "Are these all of the receipts?" He looked around and his eyes fell on our clue box.

"Yeah, that's everything since the last batch you picked up."

At that, he gathered the receipts he had spread out and put them into a pile. "I've got to get out of this town before her solicitors get to me." He looked around nervously. "You've been pestering me to sell, so here's your chance."

My heart pounded and I felt the adrenaline kick in. "Are you serious?"

"You pay me for the inventory, I'll get the papers drawn up tonight."

"That's all?" I asked with surprise. The business value was easily three times greater.

Mr. White continued shuffling paperwork. "You got it in cash?"

I nodded, thinking that between my savings and a pawn shop I'd have the money to cover the cost, though not likely a penny more.

"Good, I'll meet you here tomorrow," he said as he stuffed the receipts into a paper bag. "Don't say a word to anyone about this, you hear me?"

Mr. White snuck out of the shop quickly, as though he were being monitored. I looked around for a moment before setting up. Was the place bugged? It seemed everyone around me was acting suspiciously these days. I felt like pretty soon I really would be buying into Tony's paranoid theories.

My pulse throbbed as I realized that, on top of having to worry about being 'hunted' by our unknown assailant, I also had to come up with cash I didn't plan on needing. I impulsively answered Mr. White, but it now struck me that if I had declined, would I still have a job to go to?

The timing was way off for this venture, even though Paul and I discussed it often and wished for the chance. But now, for our sakes, I had to make it work.

Suddenly, though, my mind switched back to Mr. White's mention of Stacie. Was he involved in our whole mess? I needed to tell Mary, but it would have to wait until she was on a break.

Between tending to customers and repeatedly working out details of our night's little sting operation, I weeded through clues from our clue box. The issue of our zine had apparently ruffled quite a few feathers. Most of the comments in the box were threatening us for accusing Boise Lou. I crumpled those up and tossed them in the dustbin, but not without first appreciating that we struck a real nerve. *Scabbed Over* had gotten us a good readership!

I took notes from the other, more substantial messages, hoping some of them would lead us in the right direction. One slip of paper merely had a list of names on it: "*Stacie, Penny, Tommy, Miranda, Jules, & ?*" I recognized Tommy, Miranda, and Julie, and the order of their names mirrored the order of their deaths. Did this confirm the other clue we received, about it 'starting' with the mysterious Stacie? Who was Penny? I scribbled down my thoughts and wondered what tonight would have in store for us.

EIGHT

"Mmmm...you look good in that," Mary purred as we readied ourselves for the Clash show. Bugs had gone on a little shoplifting spree around the holidays and swiped a haphazardly-crocheted sweater from our favorite King's Road window-shopping spot. It took me a few minutes to put the damn thing on, but in the end it really did look cool.

"Now, about this shit for hair." I ran my fingers through the scrambled mess on top of my head.

Mary gave me the rest of her cigarette to smoke while she inspected my coif.

"I know!" she exclaimed and slipped away for a moment.

When she returned, she had a pair of old scissors in her hand.

"Close your eyes, luv," Mary said, snipping the air excitedly.

I did as she asked, sucking in warm smoke and twitching from the tickle of falling hairs.

Mary tugged at my disheveled hair between snips and '*hmmms*'. Once she had finished, she brushed off my face and back with her soft fingertips.

"Right. Now you can look."

It was a good thing Mary wasn't a hairdresser as the job she did on me was horrendous. My hair stuck up in varying lengths and looked worse than before she started.

"Oh! Forgot a bit!" she gasped and then quickly snipped off another piece that didn't need it. "There!"

Mary beamed, pleased with her work.

"You know, you should dye it something fun. Like...green."

I laughed. "What's wrong with having brown hair?"

She faked a dramatic yawn.

"You're just jealous because I don't have to worry about my roots growing in a different color," I teased. My fingers went for her middle, slipping beneath the hem of her equally-ragged top and finding warm skin to assail.

Mary squirmed away from me, holding her stomach. "Ugh, Jon, don't; my stomach is killing me."

"What's wrong?"

"I don't know. Nerves, probably."

I looked down at my worn-out combat boots. "Yeah, I'd be lying if I said I wasn't a little scared myself."

She bit her lip.

"But we'll have back-up," I continued, glancing back up at her. "And we've got a plan all set. It's fool-proof!"

≠

"You better keep these handy," Bugs said as he placed a couple hunting knives on his kitchen counter.

"I'm not planning on fucking *killing* anyone, Bugs," I argued.

Mary reached for a knife and tested its sharpness on her fingertip. Blood rose almost immediately from the invisible cut.

"Shit!" Mary gasped. She wrapped her finger in the hem of her skirt and held it there tightly. "I guess that wasn't too smart."

"I'm tellin' ya, Jon, you can't go wrong with one of these bastards on you." Bugs squatted down and began strapping one of the knives to my ankle.

"Where am *I* going to put one?" Mary asked.

Bugs and I looked her over, but there was no easily-accessible place on her that we could hide this size of knife.

"Here, you take this," I said, pulling my switchblade out of my pocket.

Mary snatched it greedily and stuffed it into her bra.

"You blokes will be sorry when you figure out that you should have taken this instead," Tony quipped as he entered the kitchen, exposing the gun in his jacket pocket.

This was *not* how I imagined this night starting out. "Look, maybe we should go over the plan again..."

Bugs sighed impatiently. "We got it already, Jon. I've got your back, Tony's got Mary's, and we're all watching for anything weird. So, let's shove off already!"

I clung to Mary on the way to The Rainbow, my hip still aching. It was my hope that our plan would be executed flawlessly, but at this point I was willing to accept anything that didn't involve me having to make a quick escape. I limped like my grandfather without a cane, cringing with every third step.

"You just need a few pints in you, Jonny boy," Tony commented when he saw pain on my face. "It's early days yet."

"Well, well, look who's here to greet us," Bugs remarked snidely as we approached the Rainbow Theatre. A couple of Teds were out front flanking Brody and Harlowe, Boise Lou's girlfriend.

"Pretty ballsy of them to show up in Finsbury Park, don't you think?" Tony interjected.

"I don't see Boise," I noted.

Mary peered into the group. "Don't count him out too soon. You don't really think Brody would actually be out here on his own, do you?"

"That's right, Jonny," Tony added. "That bloke's his bloody shadow."

Brody didn't make any moves. He just stood there watching us as though he were waiting for something. Harlowe leaned against a lamppost beside him and appeared to be flirting with one of the Teds in their group. Another Ted started eyeing Tony as we got in close range. I could see the blood rising in Bugs.

"Hey, remember the plan. These sods can wait," I said in an attempt to calm him down.

Bugs spat angrily at the ground, and we went inside.

The Rainbow was a fairly massive venue, compared to the usual places we saw shows. It had been a cinema at one time, but now it hosted concerts. The building seemed almost too fancy to allow punk shows, and the theatre seating, at least in my mind, presented a bit of a problem since there was no room to dance. Despite the mammoth size of the place, however, it appeared to be overflowing with people. It was going to be harder to keep track of our suspects than I originally thought with this crowd. Not to mention the fact that the place was well-stocked with bouncers.

"We'll meet here in the lobby at the breaks between sets."

Mary nodded. "Be careful, luv."

"You too," I replied, leaning in to kiss her. She held me for a minute until Bugs intruded.

"You're making me sick," he spat out. "Let's find this cunt already so I can enjoy the show."

Bugs tugged me away, pulling me deeper into the crowd towards the theater area. The Prefects were up first, and people were already buzzing. Obviously excited for the night's show, kids were bustling with energy and had started gathering in the aisles. The stage seemed monstrous compared to what we were all used to; hell, it was larger than half the pubs we knew! I could feel the anticipation of an historical night.

"We're not going to find Boise in here," Bugs yelled as we climbed through rows of seats, bumping into people in the audience.

"What if we head towards the back or to the exits? Maybe we'll run into Edwards or Jeffreys," I offered.

Bugs and I squeezed between pogo-ing punks and found our way to the back of the building. The crowd had nearly doubled since we had arrived, making it increasingly harder to find anyone. As a result, there was no sign of any of our suspects.

"So, Sherlock, what now?" Bugs grumbled. He leaned against the main staircase looking perturbed.

I hoped Mary and Tony were having better luck. Bugs was heading into one of his manic modes and I wasn't sure I could handle it. I needed a moment to think.

He began pacing. "This is bollocks! Are we just going to stand back here all night, then?"

"Wait—shut up for a second. Look over there," I pointed, spotting Gangrene. I pulled Bugs into a dark nook by the staircase so we wouldn't be seen.

"What the hell is he doing?" Bugs asked.

Gangrene slunk along the shadowy corridor as if trying to be inconspicuous, but I noticed he was frantically smoking. He glanced over his shoulder towards the lobby area repeatedly and stopped in front of a door.

"Maybe he's got a buyer?"

Through the smoky air, I saw the blackness of an opening. Gangrene leaned in against the door, pushing it. A rush of cool night air blew in and cleared some of the hazy smoke. I could make out a slender form talking to Gangrene.

"What's he saying?" I asked Bugs.

Bugs shook his head. "I'll go in closer."

I stood away from the staircase a bit, enough to give Bugs a longer shadow to hide in. He pressed himself fast against the wall and moved as close as safely possible.

One of Gangrene's hands held the door ajar while the other rummaged through his pocket. He pulled out a wad of pound notes. A gloved hand from outside took the money, then gave Gangrene a bound package.

Quickly, Gangrene looked towards the lobby. I could hear that the second band, Subway Sect, were ripping through their set, and the people in the theatre area were moving about.

Gangrene stuffed the package into his jacket. At that point, Bugs began to slide back towards me.

"Well, it was a deal alright," Bugs said as he crouched in the darkness with me. "But I could only hear what Green said. I couldn't tell who it was out there."

"Try to find that person," I replied. "I'll follow Gangrene and check in with Mary."

As soon as Gangrene stumbled off towards the lobby, Bugs and I split up. I watched Bugs sneak out the door, and I meandered through all the punks who were mingling at the bar outside the theatre area.

Gangrene settled himself against a wall and finished off a cigarette. I could tell he was trying hard to blend in with the surroundings, but in a room full of snug, mostly black clothing, his too-big jeans and baggy brown blazer stood out like a weed poking through asphalt. He was older and shaggier-looking than most of us at this show, and he seemed more lost and uncomfortable than usual.

I pushed my way through the growing crowd until I bumped into Tony and Mary.

"So, any luck?" I asked.

"None," Tony replied. "How about you?"

I told him what had just transpired with Gangrene.

He nodded. "Do you think I should go help Bugs?"

"No; he can handle himself for right now, I think. You and Mary just try to find Nige and see what he's up to. We'll meet back here at the end of the night."

It occurred to me that perhaps I could quell some of my curiosity by approaching Gangrene myself, as a mate. I was pretty sure he wasn't aware of my suspicions, so it seemed fairly safe. And if worse came to worse, I still had the knife Bugs gave me.

"Hey, Green," I greeted him when I was within hearing range.

"Jon, mate," Gangrene smiled, showing off half a mouthful of crooked teeth. "What are you doing here?"

"The same thing you're doing here," I replied.

Gangrene looked at me oddly, then his eyes shifted to each side as though to make sure someone hadn't sent me as an informant. His response was just what I was hoping for. If I could knock him off balance a little, maybe he'd slip up and tell me just what I needed to know.

"To see The Clash, of course!" I continued.

Gangrene's body relaxed a bit and he nodded. "Oh, right. The Clash." He smiled again and patted me on the shoulder, relief smoothing out the wrinkles in his brow.

"Have you seen Nige anywhere?" I asked.

Gangrene shook his head. "I've been waiting for that bastard all night. He better get to me before Boise finds him."

"Why's that?"

"Because the cunt still owes me fifty quid!"

Gangrene's eyes swept the room again quickly. The crowd had reduced by over half as the next band started banging away in the theatre. With fewer people to hide him, Gangrene became nervous again. He gave me a lame excuse about having to look for the toilet. I would have followed him, but I caught Bugs out of the corner of my eye heading towards us.

Bugs hid in the corner until Gangrene was out of sight. I noticed his lip was split once he limped over to me.

Questions spurted from my mouth the moment he came close enough: "What happened? Are you okay? Did you find him? Was it someone we knew?"

Bugs was out of breath. Blood trickled from his lip and he wiped it with the sleeve of my sweater. He steadied himself on my arm, trying to stifle his panting.

"Oh, I got to him," Bugs said coughing. "But he managed to break away."

"Well, could you see him, at least?"

He shook his head. "Nah, mate; it was too dark. I think he had a Mac on, though, because I tripped on it when I knocked him down."

Bugs coughed again, then spit blood-speckled phlegm on the floor.

"I gave him a good punch in the face, mate. Almost broke my fucking hand!" He held it up and I could see his knuckles were starting to bruise. "I swear I heard a tooth fall to the ground, but after he got away all I found were these."

He dropped into my hand a large grit-covered marble about the size of a shooter and a chewed-up pen.

"That bastard," I said, looking at the new clues. The pen confirmed my suspicions.

"Jeffreys!" Bugs exclaimed after realizing who I was referring to. "No wonder he's been after us this whole time. It would be so easy for that cunt to peg these murders on us."

"Yeah. Who would they believe: him or us?"

Bugs seethed.

"I think we need to drop in on him at the station tomorrow," I continued.

"The lovely black eye he'll have will be all we need to bust him, mate."

Jeffreys. Somehow, I just knew it. Now it was a matter of figuring out how to get Edwards to believe me. Another visit to Aunt Vi was in order, and I couldn't wait to tell Mary the news.

"Oi!" Bugs blurted out. "I hear the Buzzcocks playing. Let's catch part of the show before the sodding Jam take the stage."

We snuck into the theatre area. The crowd was on its feet, pogo-ing in the aisles and between the seats. It took all the effort security could muster to keep people from running wild in tune to the music, but for the time being there was some semblance of order. We cheered and sang along as they ripped through our favorite songs, the excitement heightening by the time they got to

"Orgasm Addict". Bugs and I spat out the lyrics feverishly with Pete Shelley as he strummed with wild abandon on his Starway: *"Sneakin' in the back door with dirty magazines and your mother wants to know 'what are those stains on your jeans?' And you're an orgasm addict!"* Despite my aching hip and Bugs' hurting leg, we found the energy to bounce along with the other sweaty kids around us.

When the Buzzcocks' set ended, Bugs and I hobbled out to the bar for a smoke, our feet crunching on discarded plastic cups. I had lost sight of Gangrene, but it seemed I had most of the answers I was looking for by that time anyway. And seeing the band took the edge off Bugs, swinging him into the calm side of his manic episode.

"Thank God!" Mary gasped, grabbing my arm. "I've been looking all over for you."

"Hey, Maire, good thing you're here. I think I've figured out…"

Mary interrupted me. "We've got a problem."

The serene look on Bugs' face began to fade. "Now what?"

"I lost Tony."

"What do you mean?" I asked.

Mary got bumped out of the way for a moment while people rushed back into the theater for The Jam, who had already started playing. Their presence on this bill seemed odd to me, considering how polished and clean-cut they and their music were. But they had a huge draw, and their energy passionately lured the crowd in. They weren't losing anyone any time soon, unlike us.

"One minute he was pointing out some bloke he thought he recognized, and then the next thing I knew, he was gone," she replied breathlessly. "I spent the last set just looking for him. I swear I've scoured this whole sodding place, but I've found nothing. No sign of him at all. It's like he was never even here."

"Bloody hell," Bugs cursed. He flicked his spent cigarette to the ground and stomped it out angrily.

"That's not all, though," Mary continued. "I found Nige, and then Gangrene caught up with him."

"What did they do?" I asked. I expected a brawl, based on my earlier meeting with Green.

"Well, they had a pretty heated conversation which ended with Gangrene storming off. But I couldn't see what happened after that because there were too many people moving around near me."

Okay, Jon. Think fast.

"Alright, Bugs...you go look for Tony. Mary and I will hunt out Nige."

Bugs nodded, then reached his hand out to me. "I need that knife, mate."

"Didn't you bring the other one?"

"Yeah, but I lost it out there. I thought I heard pigs coming, so I threw it in a bin. And when I went back, it was gone."

Mary crouched down and removed the knife, though a bit painfully, from my ankle. "I've still got your flick knife if we need it, Jon," she said as she slipped the hunting knife to Bugs.

"I'll meet you back here when I find him," Bugs said.

A blink of an eye later, he was gone.

I suggested to Mary that we start looking for Nige in the theatre area as he liked The Jam. But we didn't have to go much further than a few paces because Nige had entered the bar area with a girl on his arm. It was Harlowe.

"Shit! What does that sod think he's doing?" If Boise saw this, there would be Teds swarming the place!

Mary pulled me behind a group of smoking punks. "Shh! We can't let him know that we're spying!"

Harlowe didn't seem to care how obvious her affection was. She kissed Nige's right cheek and neck, toyed with the zippers on his leather jacket, batted her eyelashes... And to such an extreme that it looked to me like a clear trap. I could see she was trying to lead him to that door near the staircase, but he tugged her back inside the theatre area, holding the left side of his head out of fear of being seen.

"Come on, let's follow him!" I said lowly. I took Mary's hand in mine and pushed through the crowd into the theatre. Once inside, though, it was an impossible feat. The Jam had just finished whipping the crowd into a frenzy of excitement. Now, as the Clash took the stage, the audience could no longer be contained. Punks rushed up front when the first chords of "London's Burning" came bursting out. Mary and I got carried by the crowd for a few frantic moments and eventually found ourselves pressed against an outside wall. Nige was gone, Gangrene was too, and who even knew what happened to Bugs and Tony?

Suddenly, seats started flying, hurled near the stage. Fighting broke out. Joe Strummer kept singing, deep into "White Riot" while the place was being torn to shreds: *"an' everybody's doing just what they're told to, an' nobody wants to go to jail!"*

The bouncers stormed around in an attempt to restore order, but it was too late.

"...are you taking over, or are you taking orders?"

It was the best Clash performance I had thus far been to. They were truly in their element. Listening to Joe Strummer engage the audience, belting it out up there yet still one of us... it felt a bit like a revelation of my place in this society.

But, I had to break myself away—we were on a mission, after all. Mary clung to me as I slid along the wall towards an exit. I wanted to see the rest of the show, but the last thing we needed right then was to get stuck in there when the pigs arrived. We had to continue our investigation, not be trapped in someone else's. Eventually, we found our way out to the bar where Bugs said he'd meet us.

"I think I need some fresh air," Mary panted, fanning herself with her hand.

I agreed. "Bugs can meet us outside."

But as we snuck out of the theatre, we saw the lights and heard the shrill sirens of police cars. Mary pushed me up against the alley wall of a dark building nearby as the cars skidded in front of The Rainbow and cops filed out. We tried to keep as quiet as possible to not attract attention. When all the policemen had left their cars and gone inside the building, it seemed the coast was clear for us to leave.

That's when Mary screeched.

A hand had grabbed her shoulder from behind. She quickly shoved her elbow back into the person's stomach which elicited a loud, masculine groan. I jolted forward to reach for him, but my leg gave way. The pain in my hip shot up my whole side. Mary yanked at the shadowy form and slammed him against the wall. I crawled over and grabbed a foot. Then I heard Mary flick my switchblade open.

She stood there shaking, clutching my knife desperately. When she kicked the person in the groin, he crumpled over enough where I could pull him down to the ground. I punched at him, then dragged his body towards the street where we could make out his face in the light.

I had a pretty damn good idea who it would be.

My hand was raised again for another shot, but Mary dropped the knife and reached for me.

"Wait, Jon! Stop!"

NINE

"Just stand back, Maire; I've got it."

The guy on the ground squirmed and whimpered, moving his hands to his face. But when I looked down at him, I saw it wasn't Jeffreys at all. It was a curly-haired bloke in a long, now-dirty lab coat.

"Stop! It's Niall!" Mary cried. She hurried to the ground and knelt beside him, checking to see how much damage we did.

Niall held his battered head, groaning.

Slowly, I began to recognize him. It was months back when I met him, after Mary and I had taken the ferry over to Dublin to visit Keely. His younger brother Liam had been one of Mary's schoolmates.

But, what the hell was he doing here in London? And how did he find us?

Mary and I helped Niall up, and I offered him a stay at my flat for the night. It seemed the least I could do after beating the shit out of him.

He wasn't hurt enough to require a visit to the hospital, but we figured some serious rest was in order. For all of us.

There was still no sign of Bugs or Tony, but the police had begun escorting out as many of the rioters as they could fit into their cars, so Mary and I decided we'd better leave.

Mary spoke to Niall in Irish a little bit on the way back to the flat. It still seemed funny to me that I was hearing a foreign language in England, but Mary and her mates all grew up in Carraroe in County Galway, and they held fast to the language they were raised in.

We traveled slowly, hobbling all the way and hoping we wouldn't run into any Teds hungry for a row. Mary kept apologizing to Niall for the damage we caused. He leaned on my good side, which meant all of our weight rested on my hurting hip. This had been a very inconvenient week for injuries.

"Jon, the cooker's not working again," Mary called to me from the kitchen. She had started to put a pot of tea on the stove, but the pilot light must have gone out.

I was in the bedroom, madly searching for all the money I had stashed away since I moved to England. Wads of fivers and tenners were tossed on the bed as I found them in the hope that I'd have enough to pay off Mr. White in the morning. I still hadn't found the right timing to share the news with Mary, and I didn't want her to be concerned about money just yet. Not while we had Niall to worry about.

Stopping my search for the time being, I went to kitchen to see if I could get the stove going again. As I did, Mary returned to Niall with a few ice cubes wrapped in a flannel. He was laying on the couch, still holding his head.

"I'm sorry, Niall," Mary said, "but you really did scare the bloody hell out of us." She held the ice pack against his forehead.

"Caoilinn phoned me and said you'd be at The Rainbow tonight, but I didn't get a ticket in time," Niall replied softly.

"Are you the one who's been following me this past week?"

Niall nodded.

Mary sighed and rolled her eyes. "Well, why didn't you just *say* something, then? Call out my name?"

"I…well…I mean…"

"You know, Niall, you're the complete opposite of your brother. He'd have put on a public performance to get my attention."

He shot a slightly embarrassed look at her, then cast his eyes away with a half-smile.

Niall was lucky I had given Bugs back his knife before we ran into him. I shivered to think of what I might have done with it.

The flame finally flickered on after toying with the stove's knobs a bit, and I prepared the tea for us.

"So, what brings you all the way to London, Niall?" I asked while pulling a tin of tea out of the cupboard. My head pounded from the evening's adventure, and I couldn't wait to just relax with my friends.

"I'm here at university, in the medical college," he said.

"Oh, yeah? What's that like, then?"

Niall shrugged. "It's alright, I guess. Right now I'm stuck doing all the dirty jobs. I get to clean the anatomy labs after sessions and transfer donations."

"Donations?" Mary asked.

"Research donations. *Cadavers*, I mean."

Mary wrinkled her nose.

"I think I've seen all the stiffs I want to for a while," I said a bit smartly. My hands reached for something insulated to carry the tea kettle over to the living room. I noticed I was shaking a little.

Mary glanced over at me. "Jon, someone needs to teach you how to make tea."

"What are you talking about?"

"You bring the cups to the kettle, not the kettle to the cups!" She gave me a scolding look.

"That's what I wanted to talk to you about," Niall said, pulling himself up to a sitting position and placing the ice pack on an end table.

"Niall, you've *never* made tea for..." Mary chided him before he cut her off.

"No, the bodies. Susan..."

Mary bit her lip and I stopped what I was doing to give him my full attention.

"I had to find you, Maire. In case I got in trouble. So you'd know." He stopped for a moment to gather his thoughts.

"When I heard about her, I couldn't believe it. I had to see her," Niall continued. "The toxicology tests hadn't even been done yet, but her cause of death was already listed as 'suicide' on the coroner's report."

"But, the inquest?" Mary interjected.

"That's just it...one wasn't even opened."

She shook her head in disbelief. "How could that be?"

I didn't really know how these things worked yet in England, but it soon became obvious by Mary's back-and-forth with Niall that this wasn't typical protocol.

"Listen to me, Maire. I took a sample. When I was there for a donation, I snuck a blood sample before her post-mortem."

Mary shook her head again. "Niall, they're going to know. They'll see the mark, know it was done *after* she was dead."

"I had to know. I thought she was poisoned. I was sure I'd find something I could trace or recreate in the lab. But what I found was pure. Absolutely pure heroin."

"She couldn't have gotten that. Not on these streets, and not from Gangrene," I argued. "He can't afford not to split his stuff."

"I need to get into the files," Niall said, a rising nervousness in his voice. "And... I need your help."

We all looked at each other in silence for a moment, scared at what this might mean.

"Right," I finally said, holding my hand out to him. Niall took it firmly.

"This is what we know..."

Mary and I shared with him the clues from our clue box. Niall had no idea who Stacie was, but his plan was to go through coroner's reports of the deaths we did know about to see what kind of connections we could find. I had no idea how he'd get away with this or what to do if he didn't. But, we were in it together.

Mr. White was waiting impatiently for me at Beaufort Market in the morning. A couple cigarette butts were smashed at his feet, like he'd been there for hours even though the sun had risen not more than thirty minutes ago. None of the other shopkeepers had arrived yet, either.

"You got the money?" Mr. White asked hurriedly, his eyes sweeping over the street like he was engaging in a drug deal.

I reached in my pocket and handed him a wad of cash. "This is all of it. 769 pounds. My savings and everything."

His lips wrinkled and his hands shook as he flipped though the bills. "Well, that'll have to do," he replied, agitated. He felt around his pockets and handed me various creased and folded forms, each not-so-carefully embossed with a notary seal that was certainly forged. Then, dropping a set of keys into my hand, he patted me on the shoulder, wished me well, and slunk away down the street.

So, just like that, I had the shop. Deep down, it was what I always wanted, but the timing was way off. I wasn't sure I even knew what the hell I was supposed to do. When I went inside and inspected the paperwork Mr. White gave me, I saw that it had all been back-dated to look as though our transaction took place months ago. Thankfully, the rent to Beaufort Market for our space was low, and the next payment wasn't due for a few more weeks. However, as I began readying the shop for customers, I discovered the catch: Mr. White had cleaned out the contents of the till, all 137 pounds' worth. He even took the pence pieces out of the drawer. Now I had to start from scratch, and since I had just withdrawn all my savings to give to him, I had nothing left.

I tried aggressively to sell as much as I could that day in the hope of replenishing the money Mr. White took, as well as having a spot of cash for Mary and I to survive on the next week. I spent down-time thinking of new articles for the next issue of our zine. Our investigation needed to move faster. The killer was still loose and any one of us could be his next target.

My thoughts went to Paul. The hospital hadn't phoned me yet to report on his condition, but I didn't want to wait. After closing up for the day, I stopped there. The barbed-wire I wore around my wrist gave security something to fuss over for a bit, but eventually I was escorted upstairs to Paul's room.

As I entered, however, I found that Paul was not alone. Leaning over him was none other than Jeffreys, dressed in a constable's uniform. My escort left me there with my mouth gaping at Paul's company. There would be no need for me to go to the police station now; my evidence was standing fifteen feet away. But, what on earth was he doing here?

Jeffreys looked up to see me, suddenly adjusting the blanket tucked around Paul's motionless body. Momentary surprise flickered across his face as I stepped into the room.

Clearing my throat, I said, "I didn't expect to see you here."

"Yeah, well, I thought I'd check up on your friend before I finished some paperwork." He pulled out a pen and chewed on it nervously. *What the fuck had I just interrupted?*

I decided it would be more advantageous to just play along. "Has he come 'round yet?"

Jeffreys shook his head. "Not since I've been here."

Stepping closer to the bed, I looked at Jeffrey's face. I anticipated the damage Bugs had inflicted upon him in the alley last night. My pulse quickened. What would I do when I found my proof?

But what I found instead was his normal, freckled skin; no sign of any bruising, no missing teeth, no black eye, not even razor burn from the morning's shave. Surely, he couldn't have healed overnight.

"What's that for, then?" Jeffreys asked me, his eyes narrowing.

I blinked myself back into the moment. "What?"

"Why are you looking at me like that?" He stopped chewing on his pen.

I held my hands up. "I'm just tired, that's all. I didn't mean anything by it."

Jeffreys pointed his pen at me for a quick second before putting it back into his mouth.

"I was going to stop at the station," I blurted out to ease the tension. The absence of evidence I found on Jeffreys' face had thrown me for a loop. "I might have some information that Edwards could use."

"Well, you're going to have to settle for me instead because he's not in tonight."

I raised my eyebrow at him. How convenient Edwards' absence was.

Jeffreys frowned. "You little sods think we sit on our arses all day twiddling our thumbs. How can we when we have to be out chasing after bastards like you? I haven't had a holiday in months!"

I backed off a bit, seeing as I obviously hit a nerve.

"Now's his go. So if you've got something to say, you're bloody well going to have to say it to *me*."

As I was pondering whether I'd even bother now, the crackle of Jeffreys' radio diverted his attention.

"Right. I'm on my way," he replied to the voice on the other end. He rushed past me without saying another word, his footsteps echoing through the corridor until he disappeared down a staircase.

"*Well, now what?*" I asked Paul's silent form. He laid there like a mummy, still hidden beneath gauze.

It had turned into a night that deserved a few pints, but I knew I ought to get home to Mary. I still hadn't mentioned anything to her about the record store, which was sure to cheer her up.

Teds were out that night lining King's Road, but none of them made a move on me. They rested against storefronts simply watching as I walked past. I shoved my hands into my pockets and headed towards the tube station as quickly as I could to avoid any possible confrontations. Once I arrived at Sloane Square, however, I realized I had stayed at the hospital too long and would have to wait a while for the next train. I thought of Tommy and what he must have looked like to the sorry sod who found him in the bin.

Then my thoughts shifted to Boise Lou and his curious absence last night.

But, suddenly, something behind me rustled in the shrubbery.

I jumped up off the bench I was sitting on, startled. My hand went instinctively to my trouser pocket for my switchblade, but I forgot Mary had taken it.

"*Pssst, Jon, mate,*" a voice whispered from the shadows.

"Who the fuck...?"

"*It's me, Nige.*"

I saw his head peek out of the darkness momentarily to see if the spot was safe.

"What the hell are you doing?" I asked him, shaking from the scare.

"What does it *look* like I'm doing?"

"It looks like you're being a stupid cunt," I snapped back.

"Fine. Shove off, then. I don't need attention drawn to me right now." He pulled his head back into the shrubbery a bit.

"This wouldn't have anything to do with last night, would it?"

There was silence for a moment.

"What are you talking about?" Nige asked. His voice quivered.

"I saw you with Harlowe, man. What were you thinking?"

Nige climbed out of his hiding spot, brushing twigs and leaves out of his clothes. "I happen to like her, alright?" He stood in the shadows, but enough light from the street trickled in that I could see his left eye was all puffy and purple.

"What happened to *you*?"

"Some bloke just hauled off and hit me last night, is all," Nige grumbled.

When I peered in closer I saw that a tooth had been knocked loose, too.

"A bloke? What for?" Something definitely wasn't right here. Maybe I had been looking at this puzzle all wrong. Tony's paranoid theory was becoming less absurd by the minute.

"I don't know...just a miscommunication." He fidgeted with something in his pocket. "It was pretty wild last night, eh? What about that riot?"

I shrugged, but my mind was racing. I had to talk to Tony and find out what else he saw. I had to get back to Mary and look at those clues again. And I had to visit Aunt Vi to see if it could all be put together.

"You haven't seen Boise around here, have you?" Nige looked around nervously.

I closed my eyes and shook my head. The phantom sound of the train whispered its way closer and closer, promising me I'd be home-sweet-home soon. When my eyelids opened, Nige was gone.

The tube ride lasted for what seemed like hours. Sitting so long made the pain in my hip shoot straight up my spine. I dreamed of how wonderful it would feel to curl up in my enveloping couch, a cigarette in one hand, a pint in the other, and Mary snuggled against me. We could write more articles for our zine aloud, study our clues, put our intellect to the test. I had a tingly feeling that the answer to this mystery was within reach, if only I could think through it all logically.

I started to feel some luck coming on when I entered Farringdon Towers and found that the lift was finally up and running. That had to be a sign of things to come. Now, if only I hadn't left my cigarettes with Mary as well...

A smile crept across my face as I approached the door to my flat, feeling the nervous excitement rising over getting to tell Mary about Fresh Slab. But as I turned the doorknob, I could hear the angry sound of her cursing.

TEN

My eyes widened as I opened the door. There was Mary on her knees, crying in the middle of the living room. The contents of my flat were strewn around her all helter-skelter, clothes mixed with broken crockery, scattered amongst shreds of newspaper. It was as if a tornado had hit.

I rushed down to Mary and took her in my arms tightly, my heart now racing in unadulterated fear. She clenched me.

"The door was unlocked when I came home from the pub," she sniffled. "And then I saw this." Her hand motioned to the mess.

"Were you here long?"

"No, I just walked in about ten minutes ago."

I wiped the tears off her cheeks with my thumb.

"Jon, I don't think it was a burglar."

I looked around and saw that the furniture had been upturned, drawers had been emptied, papers had been rifled through.

"I checked the bedroom first," Mary continued, "and all the rent money I left on the chest of drawers yesterday is still there, in plain view."

"Anything expensive taken? Like my record player, maybe?"

Mary pointed to the floor in the corner where my record player had been deposited.

I stifled a growl. Random violence I could accept, but this... Someone was looking for something in particular, and I hoped that whatever it was, they hadn't found it.

We cleaned up the mess as best we could, moving papers into piles, separating out shards of anything shattered, and folding up clothing. A few things had been broken, particularly cups and saucers, but nothing appeared to be missing.

"What could they have been looking for, then?" Mary asked, wiping her dusty hands on her lap.

I didn't know.

"I'm nervous, Jon. Should we even stay here tonight?" Her eyes looked at me pleadingly.

"I'll call Bugs and Tony," I replied in agreement. My fingers went to her face gently. "I need to talk to Tony anyway."

On about the seventh ring, Tony finally picked up. I could hear Bugs yelling in the background, making a real fuss.

"What's his problem?" I asked.

Tony shouted something to him, his hand muffling the receiver, before responding. "Some bastard trashed the place, mate. They must have waited til Gusty and the boys upstairs were out."

"Maire, they hit Bugs and Tony, too!" I called out.

Mary rushed over to me to listen in on the conversation.

"Someone tore up our place today as well, man," I replied to Tony.

Mary crossed her arms and stood next to me, the look on her face betraying her thoughts. We weren't safe anywhere until this bastard was caught.

"I'm tellin' ya, Jonny boy," Tony said, "we've got to go after Nige. That fucking cunt's up to no good!"

"I ran into him tonight on my way home. He was hiding at Sloane Square with the biggest black eye I ever saw." I paused for a minute.

"Are you thinking what I'm thinking?" Tony asked.

"If you're thinking that maybe Nige is the bloke Bugs roughed up at the show, then yeah."

Tony cleared his throat.

"What is going on with him?" I asked rhetorically.

"He had a row with some bint early on last night, during Subway Sect, I think. I tried to follow her after he took off, but by the end of the night I gave up."

"I just wish I knew what was going through his mind."

Tony grumbled something about Julie, then mentioned Susan sadly. He had managed to visit her grave site earlier in the day but was still upset that we had been barred from the funeral.

"All we owe her family is the truth, Tony. And we'll have it soon."

I hung up with him, not feeling any more secure over our situation than before I phoned. It was too late to ring Aunt Vi, so I made the decision to stay at the flat.

"Well, I can't change the lock until tomorrow since the shops are all closed by now, but maybe we can at least rig something so that we'll be safe inside."

Mary helped me transform the barbed wire on my wrist into an additional chain around the door lock so that, if pried open, the door wouldn't budge far enough to cut the link. It didn't look too sturdy, but we prayed it would hold.

"Maybe they were looking for these," Mary said as she brought out an old tin. She tilted the can over and dumped out all the clues we had gathered, including the ones Bugs had given me last night.

"I think we should give this to Niall to see if he can tell us what was injected with it." I held up the broken syringe needle we found at the scene of Susan's attack.

Mary agreed and separated out the two chewed pens, both tell-tale markings of Jeffreys.

"I don't know, Jon," Mary said while inspecting them. "That's just too obvious, don't you think?"

"Yeah, but he's been suspicious from day one. You can't deny that."

Mary shrugged. "Well, what about this, then?" She rolled the marble in her palm, inspecting it.

"I guess if you threw it at someone hard enough it could hurt them pretty badly."

"Or maybe if you rolled it on the ground you could trip someone, break an ankle?" Mary offered.

We stared at the object, coming up with only the most outlandish uses for it.

"It could just be trash," I said finally.

She nodded and placed everything back into the tin except the needle. We'd pass that on to Niall tomorrow.

"Well, I *did* have some better news when I came home," I said to Mary when we were finally in bed.

She followed the outline of a small tattoo on my chest with her fingernails. "About Paul?" Her voice perked up.

"No; no news yet on him," I answered. "It's about Fresh Slab."

I picked at her hair, toying with the new tangles I helped create fifteen minutes earlier.

Mary nibbled on my shoulder blade. "Oh?"

"You're looking at the new owner."

"Are you serious?" Mary gasped. "That's wonderful, luv!"

I felt warm skin against mine as she nestled against me, leaning in to kiss me full on the mouth.

"I just don't know if we'll be able to stay afloat. I mean, I didn't expect this so suddenly, without warning. I gave him every cent I had."

"We've made it work before, Jon. I'll put in more hours at the pub if I have to."

I frowned slightly.

"Don't worry, luv. We'll be all right."

Mary's lips went to my ear lobe. The heat of her breath made my skin twitch. I wanted to pull her tightly against me, slip myself back inside her, show her just how much I truly loved her... but all that came out was a long, pleasured sigh. Her hands stroked the length of me, gently at first then more fevered with my deepening breath. Just as I felt the warmth of orgasm start to wash over me, Mary stopped.

"Jon, what if Mr. White has something to do with the murders?" she stammered, as though the realization just hit her.

I whimpered at her timing. Couldn't that have waited another minute?

My body shuddered off the sensation, and I slowly caught my breath, pain lingering between my legs.

Mary rolled onto her back, resting her head in the crook of my arm. She stared at the ceiling momentarily, collecting her thoughts.

"Maybe he figured out we were close to breaking the case?" she finally suggested.

My fingers rested along the curve of her breast, massaging her skin gently. "We're not *that* close, Maire," I replied. "Besides, what would *he* gain from any of it?"

She nuzzled me. "Well, don't you think that everything would fall into place if we knew the answers to only a couple more questions?"

I considered her observation. "Who is Stacie?"

Mary nodded into my chest. "That's one."

"If there's another, I really think it has to do with Gangrene's dealer."

"Or Nige's connection to this whole mess."

"And what about Jeffreys and Edwards?"

"I don't know, Jon. What benefit would it get them? None of the people killed were criminals or dealers, so why would they bother?"

I tickled Mary's side gently. "See? We've still got too many questions that haven't been answered. Plus, what about Boise? There's no way he's blameless."

Mary wrapped one of her legs over mine. "Boise may be a bastard, but I don't think he's that daft; he'd know we'd find him out straight away."

"Well, I still think I should follow him around a while. I want to see what part he's played in all this."

Mary sighed and pressed her lips to my chest for another kiss. She pulled me close, curling herself against me warmly, temporarily shutting down my over-analytical mind. A bit of calm washed over me, and despite this evening's drama, I couldn't help but smile.

≠

"Jonathan, don't dawdle," Aunt Vi said as she waved me into her house the next evening.

Mary had gone to the university with Niall to test the needle we found, and I decided to head over to Aunt Vi's for any juicy gossip that might lead to a clue.

"You haven't gotten in trouble with the police again, have you?" Aunt Vi asked as she placed a tray of biscuits in front of me.

"No, why?"

She set out a cup of tea for me before sitting down. "The Chief Inspector stopped by for a moment this morning and seemed concerned about you."

My mouth opened to reply when she continued: "And I've read in the paper about this recent unpleasantness. Really, Jonathan, you should know better than to carry on with such *dreadful* people." She shook her head sadly and reached for a biscuit.

"He's such a pleasant man," Aunt Vi sighed

as she went back to talking about the Chief Inspector. "And he treats his wife as if she were the Queen Herself. What he wouldn't do for her!" She smiled, taking a nibble of her biscuit. Her eyes stared at nothing, like in a daydream. "He reminds me of your uncle sometimes, God bless him."

I never knew him as he died when I was just a child, but Uncle Albert had been a fairly high-ranking official in the Royal Army. Aunt Vi had little to worry about financially since Uncle Albert had left her a nice estate, so she didn't need to forge a living for herself. Instead, she made it her occupation to concern herself with the neighbors' lives.

"Why, he's taken her on a trip to the Cotswolds. It's such a lovely tour. Perhaps I'll take one later this year. You *know* how miserable London becomes in the winter. Miriam told me that the last time she went on holiday, she stayed at a delightful manor home in Cheltenham. Tea in the garden every day for a week! Why, even Dr. Singleton said..."

I ate a couple biscuits while my aunt continued, trying not to get crumbs all over her carpet. She was clearly infatuated with Edwards, and I couldn't see what the big deal was other than the fact that he had a notorious job.

"I wonder why the Chief Inspector stops by here to check up on me?" I asked suddenly. Aunt Vi stopped her daydream and I realized that my rhetorical question was said not in my head but aloud.

"Well, of course he's concerned about you, dear," Aunt Vi answered. "He's always checked in on us. He saved your uncle's life in the war, you know."

I cocked my head at her.

"If Albert hadn't gone to his infirmary, who knows if he would have survived with all that shrapnel. A fine medic he was. Such a fine man." She beamed and took a satisfied sip of her tea.

I guess I could give up the hope that Edwards might stop following my movements now that I understood his connection to my aunt. I wasn't sure the information I gleaned from Aunt Vi was relevant at all, other than confirmation that Edwards was, in fact, out of London for a while. Well, that and perhaps the suggestion that he was more likely our guardian angel than evil culprit.

Mary added something else to the mix, though.

"We found our own interesting information," she said to me when I returned home. She and Niall were having dinner at the kitchen table.

Niall put down his fork. "The needle's clean, Jon."

"What?"

"It was either accidentally dropped there…"

"…or someone planted it there knowing we'd find it," Mary interrupted.

I thought for a moment. "So, it's possible that our other clues could be fakes as well."

Mary nodded.

"Lots of things get tossed in alleys, Jon," Niall replied. "I'm not saying this can't be an important clue; I'm just saying that it was still sterile when it fell there."

I frowned. That wasn't getting us anywhere. "Any luck with that list of names we gave you?" I lit a cigarette and helped myself to what was left on the stove.

Niall nodded. "There's a cover-up. There's got to be."

"Listen to this," Mary interjected.

Niall continued: "I didn't get to everyone. Without surnames or dates, I didn't have enough time to find anything on Stacie or Penny. Tommy's file was there, but the pathologist's report was missing."

"An inquest can't still be open on him, right?" Mary asked. From what her friends said when we were down in Crawley, it seemed that at least his case was being treated as something suspicious since he had also been beaten.

"Right. It seems too long to have an open inquest. Miranda's and Julie's deaths have already been registered," Niall said, taking a swig of ale.

"What does that mean?" I asked honestly.

"That means the coroner signed off on the post-mortems without inquests, most likely. If he had ordered inquests, there's no way they would be registered already; it takes longer than this to do it properly."

I picked at the bread on my plate. "So, now what?"

Mary looked at Niall, biting her lip.

"I... I think I need to have another go at it. I've got to see Susan's file."

"No, that's far too risky," Mary protested.

"It's not like I'm going to nick it," Niall retorted.

A sly smile grew slowly across my face.

"Jon, no," Mary said as she noticed me. "That's crazy."

Niall's eyes glittered. "Fancy being a lab assistant?"

"Aunt Vi always wanted me to go to university," I winked.

Mary put her hand to her head in defeat.

When Niall left, Mary and I began piecing together a new issue of our zine. *The Real White Riot*, Mary titled her feature article. In it she described the murders of our mates. We hoped that by being so honest it would cause someone to come forward with additional information. Or perhaps it would scare the perpetrator into confessing when he discovered that we knew the deaths were not accidental.

"We *must* be getting close, Maire," I said from the floor. I was engaged in my official role of cover-art designer by snipping through the day's newspaper for good collage material. "And the culprit has got to be someone we know. It would be too coincidental for Bugs and Tony to have their flat torn apart the same day as ours and with nothing even stolen."

"I agree." Mary's fingernails clicked against the typewriter keys. "Whoever it is must know we're on their trail."

I started pasting letters onto a blank piece of paper. "I was thinking, maybe I should pay Gangrene a visit."

"Do you even know where he is?"

"Yeah, he's squatting at a flat in Aylesbury Street this week. Or, at least, that's what Tony told me."

Mary pulled her finished article out of the typewriter. "I don't know, Jon. That guy is bad news. I mean, if he's got anything to do with this mess, I don't want you there alone with him."

"Maybe Bugs will come with me?"

Mary put another piece of paper in the typewriter. "I just don't feel good about it."

"Look, we've *got* to find out what he knows about this. Who is he buying from? What part is he playing?"

I gave Mary the cover I made. She took a deep breath, then stood up before me.

"Well, if you're that serious about it, *I'm* going with you."

"No," I began, but Mary put her hand over my mouth.

"You're stuck with me, whether you like it or not." She rested her hands on her hips and wouldn't budge.

There was no way I could talk Mary out of it now. And, as usual, she was right; I'd never be able to do this without her.

≠

Mary had the next issue of our zine printed in the morning. There were a few sales by the time I closed up the shop, but our clue box remained empty.

Before heading home, we decided to visit Paul at St. Stephen's to check on his recovery.

"Hey, that looks like Jeffreys," I said, my hand jutting out to point at a uniformed man leaving the building from a back exit.

Mary looked at me curiously. "What would *he* be doing here?"

I shrugged. "I don't know. He was here yesterday when I stopped by. I saw him leaning over Paul, and it looked pretty suspicious."

Mary's brow furrowed with a passing thought, but she said nothing.

"His condition is improving," the nurse tending to Paul said to us when we reached his room, "but he hasn't opened his eyes yet." She tidied up the tubes attached to him. "He's responded to certain stimuli, though, which is a very good sign." The woman smiled, trying to lighten our moods.

"Did a police officer just leave here?" Mary inquired. She stroked Paul's hand gently.

The nurse nodded. "Detective Inspector Jeffreys was just in."

"I wonder what would make him come to see Paul?" I said, not meaning for it to be so audible.

"Well, if it weren't for the Inspector, we may have arrived for your friend too late. He was the one who radioed in to us."

She smiled again then left the room.

Mary cocked her head. "See, maybe he's not such a bad guy after all."

I pursed my lips, weighing the evidence. "That's not to say he didn't do the damage himself, then called it in to make it look like someone else was the attacker."

I wish I could talk to Edwards, I thought to myself. My gut feeling was that he knew something which would tie the ends of this mystery together, especially if my aunt was right about his concern.

We stayed with Paul a little while longer, then decided it was time to head home. Sleep was the only thing that could help clear our minds.

But it wouldn't come soon enough.

As we turned down a corridor to leave, we ran into a hobbling Gangrene. His leg was set in a cast, and he was attempting to walk with crutches.

ELEVEN

"Jon, mate! Mary!" Gangrene exclaimed. He grinned wide, exposing a dentist's nightmare.

"What happened to *you*?" Mary asked him.

He looked down at his cast. "Some fucking Teddy cunt knifed me at The Rainbow the other night." His voice sounded strange without the slur of alcohol. "What are you doing here?"

"We stopped to see Paul," I replied.

Gangrene leaned against his crutches, wobbling. "Paul works here, too?" He blinked confusedly.

I sighed and explained what happened to Paul. Gangrene acted completely oblivious to the incident.

Mary and I helped him out to the street, making small talk. He was going to take a bus back to the flat he was staying at, so we decided to keep him company as he waited. Now was the time to interrogate him, while he was still sober.

"Hey, Green, do you know anyone named Stacie?"

"Yeah, why?"

Mary looked at me with urging eyes to make something up.

"What's she like?" I asked dumbly. Mary shoved an elbow into my side, but all I could do was shrug and hope he didn't notice.

Gangrene stared into the street, looking for the bus. "Rich little twat. Needs to learn some manners."

"Do you see her often?" Mary asked.

He shook his head. "Only when she needs a hook-up."

I looked around to be sure no cops were near enough to hear us; we didn't have time to be thrown in jail on drug-trafficking charges.

"I haven't seen her in a while, though," Gangrene continued. "I'll give her *what for* if I find out she's buying straight from my new guy."

Mary and I glanced at each other quickly while Gangrene felt around his pockets for bus fare.

"You've got a new supplier?" Mary asked as innocently as possible.

He waved at an oncoming red bus. "Yeah."

"Is he...uh...nice?" I stuttered.

Gangrene's eyes peered at me suspiciously. "*Nice*?"

The bus slowed and stopped before us.

"I've never actually seen the bloke," he replied, pulling himself up into the bus. He didn't bother looking back at us once the bus accelerated away.

"Well, that was interesting," Mary said plainly.

We stood there for a moment, watching the lights of the bus become red dots that disappeared into the darkness.

"What do you think?" I asked.

Mary shook her head. "I don't know. He's just so...careless about it all."

"I should follow him..."

Mary's hand reached out for my arm. "No. Not yet, at least. We need a plan first."

"I think we should definitely keep with our Stacie investigation," Mary said as she tied her hair up. "Something tells me that clue isn't a joke."

She stood beside me, completely naked. "Well?"

I glanced up at her from the floor. Random nail clippings and other such unvacuumed remains poked into my bare skin.

"Am I gonna just stand here like this all night, or are you gonna do something about it?" A bead of perspiration slowly crawled its way over the curve of her breast then dropped like desire onto my leg. She was close enough that I could almost taste the saltiness of her.

"Look, I'm trying, okay?" I replied breathlessly. My hands fumbled with a pipe wrench in an attempt to turn the radiator off. The apartment had become a sauna.

I kept losing my grip as my hands were sweating. Nothing seemed to work until I started using the wrench like a mallet, hammering the stubborn valve with it. Steam burst out for a moment, then slowed to a fading mist. Mary and I stared at the cursed thing until it became completely silent.

"Well, they say this is supposed to do wonders for our skin, at least," I offered as I rolled over slowly, aching from the effort in the thick air.

"Yeah?" Mary put her hands on her hips defiantly. Her freckled flesh was blotchy from the extreme humidity. "Well, they can piss off!"

"I'm going to try to find out more about Gangrene's dealer. That's got to play a part in all this, don't you think?"

"Yeah, it might," Mary replied.

I groaned as her elbow dug into my groin.

"Can you stretch your leg out a little more?" she asked. Her body was wedged against mine in the cool water of the bath.

I wiggled a bit, hitting my head against the tile wall. Crumbled grout speckled the water for a brief moment, then disappeared to someplace beneath us. "I don't think this thing was meant for two." The back of my head throbbed, and I knew we'd have muscle cramps like rigor mortis in the morning, but it was all we could think of to keep ourselves from passing out from the apartment's heat.

Mary relaxed a bit against me and a few minutes later her breathing became regular. I was too exhausted to move any more, so we fell asleep there, not waking until we had become prunes the next morning.

≠

"Sorry to hear about your mate, Hunter," Boise Lou said, confronting me as I left McSurley's on my lunch hour.

"Yeah, it's too bad," Brody chimed in.

Boise's lips curled into a sly smile.

I could feel bile rising in my throat. My hands went out and shoved Boise. "And what do you know about it, you cunt?"

Boise shoved back, planting me against the brick façade of the building. "A little *bird* told me." He chuckled softly. Brody echoed him.

"If you laid a hand on him…" I spat out, but Boise shook his head.

"I told you he should watch himself, Hunter. Too bad the bloke who roughed him up didn't leave anything for *me*."

My fist shot out and cracked him in the jaw. He stumbled back a couple steps but was steadied by Brody.

Boise rubbed at his face. "You ought to be more careful." His finger pointed at me as I retreated towards Beaufort Market. "Never leave a job unfinished, Hunter. You'll come to regret it."

≠

"Jon! Jon!"

Mary's voice pierced through layers of dust on album sleeves to reach me in Fresh Slab later that afternoon. She ran in, pulling me aside.

"What the hell..."

"Jon, I think you're right," Mary panted. "I just talked to Carol, and she said that she never knew Harlowe's real name..."

"Well, how does *that* help us?"

"Don't you see?" Mary asked. "She could be the Stacie we're looking for!"

I glanced up out of the stall to see Carol looking back at me. But when my eyes caught hers, she blended back into the clothes in her shop.

"We've got to find her," Mary continued. "And we never did find out where Boise was that night, did we?"

I shook my head. "Not unless Tony did and just didn't tell us."

Mary sighed. "If only Paul could talk to us."

My lips tightened into a frown.

When we arrived at St. Stephen's a little while later, the doctor had some good news—Paul had come out of his coma.

Mary ran to Paul's bed excitedly, but the doctor reached for her. "He really ought to rest. We're still not sure yet how much damage was incurred by him being unconscious for so long."

"Has he said anything to you?" I asked.

The doctor shook his head. "But, his eyes seem to be able to follow us around the room, and he responds reflexively to his name." He smiled at us proudly.

Mary was so happy that she leaned in and planted a big kiss on the doctor's cheek.

He blushed and tried to compose himself quickly. I snickered to myself. Mary's red lipstick stood out on his face like an open wound.

"Well, then," the doctor stammered. "I'd better get back to work."

Mary winked at me as he slipped out of the room with a renewed sense of urgency.

Hope welled up inside me, and I pulled Mary close. Maybe the end would come soon, after all?

"See?" she whispered in my ear. "We'll have our answers in no time."

"Bloody hell…"

"No, it's right, it's right."

"I feel like a poofter."

"Just… stay near me and you'll be fine."

Niall and I walked down the corridor with purpose. He held a clipboard with paperwork for a donation he was arranging to claim. I kept by his side, appearing as his assistant in a matching university lab coat and false identification badge. This was the moment of truth.

Our footsteps echoed through the long hallway. Niall picked a time of day when the coroner's office was relatively light of employees–file clerks at lunch, coroner's officers at police stations, visitors non-existent. It was going to be quick and easy.

"Okay, I think we should split up," Niall said, glancing up and down the hall, surveying the various closed doors.

"What exactly am I looking for?"

"The coroner's files are in these two areas." Niall motioned to two rooms on our left. "I need to see what is in Susan's file. Search everything you can."

I nodded, feeling around in my pockets for my cigarettes.

"And, for God's sake, don't make a scene," he said, grasping my shoulder.

"Where are you off to, then?"

Niall gestured down the hall to the right. "I'm going straight to the surgery."

"Eh?"

"The operating theatre."

I narrowed my eyes at him.

"To the bodies."

He glanced at the doors and continued: "I want to find the pathologist. I... I need to check on something. Just meet me back at the lorry."

Niall slipped down the hall quickly while I snuck into the first room. The lights were out and I thought it best to keep it that way. Tall filing cabinets lined the walls. The glow from the hallway lit the cabinet labels just enough for me to squint and situate myself. In the middle of the room was an uncluttered steel desk. Another door led out the back of the room into a lit area; it was slightly ajar and looked like a great escape route if I ended up needing one.

It took me some time to figure out the filing arrangement. I had to duck from passers-by a few times and almost risked discovery when a new clerk nudged the light switch on after entering mistakenly, thinking she had found the break room. When I regained my composure, I got to work on locating the drawer Susan's paperwork might be in. Flicking my lighter briefly, I searched.

'77. The B's. B-a, B-e, B-i, B-o... Boardman, Bolton, Bonder, Booth, Botsam, Bowers, Bowman... Susan Bowman.
I snatched the file from the cabinet greedily and tore through the pages to be sure I had the correct person. Polaroid photos of the body fell from the folder and my heart dropped with them. It was the right file.

But as I crouched to the floor to gather the loose evidence, I could hear voices approaching the back door area. I scurried behind the desk.

Two figures stood near the doorway, continuing their conversation. I couldn't make out faces, but one of the voices seemed familiar. Muffled, I heard only parts of the discussion:

"It's a sad affair."
"...soon..."
"What about him, then?"
"...expect more bodies..."
"But, you'll have it."
"...clean, no worries."
"File it before six. Seven?"
"Six. It's signed."
"...and then?"
"I promise."

When the talking moved closer, I shoved Susan's file into my shirt, pulled the lab coat tight against me, and skidded to the hallway door. My breath held tight, I jiggled the handle just enough to open the door a crack and roll out before the two figures could know there had been an intruder. A secretary passed by me as I was panting in the corridor, a quizzical look on her face.

"Sorry. Asthma," I replied, getting up.

She wrinkled her face at me and quickened her pace.

Right.

I walked out with determination and focus, hoping to avoid any further suspicion.

Niall was waiting nervously for me in the transport truck.

"What happened?" he asked, his eyes darting around. "I almost went back in after you." He began to put the vehicle in gear. "Do you have the form?"

I pulled the crumpled file from my clothes.

Niall's eyes widened. "Not the whole bloody file!" He looked around desperately at the entrance of the building. "Now they'll know we're up to something! They'll find us!"

"Bollocks. Just drive."

He gave me a panicked look and stalled.

"Damn it, go!" I stomped my foot over his onto the gas pedal.

The truck lurched forward and Niall took over, seeing that I was serious. He drove off toward the university.

"This is *so* illegal, Jon. This is.. It's... trespassing and thievery and spying and..." The reality of what we did was hitting Niall, but I was having none of it.

"Oh, piss off. You said you needed more info. Well, here it is. You can't just back out now that you got what you wanted."

"But, with the *whole* file gone... that's not just a misplaced document. It's obvious. And... what are we going to do if we *do* find something in it? If we tell anyone, they'll know it was us that took it."

"Yeah, well, we can worry about that later, then. First we have to figure out what's going on so we can try to stop it from happening again."

"So, what is it that you were looking for?" I asked Niall once we were in his lab. I had just finished helping him transfer and store the donation he picked up from the coroner, and now we were sitting among beakers and test tubes, Susan's file spread out on the counter before us.

Niall rifled through the papers. "This," he replied, pulling out the pathologist's report. But, instead of inspecting the results, he began to study the form itself.

"The handwriting. The pathologist is the same one that did Tommy's and Julie's reports," he continued, pointing at the signature at the bottom. "A cursive 'M. U.' I don't know anyone there with a surname beginning with 'U'."

I looked at the paper again, frowning at the description of the body. Niall found the Polaroids and stared at them sadly for a few moments.

"I saw an unusual bloke talking to the coroner when I went to get the donation," he finally said. "Had an eye patch."

"What?"

"Never saw him there before, but seemed to know what he was doing. Still, kind of funny. Like a pirate guarding his treasure. Took a while to get the body with him talking so much. Nice pirate, though."

Our discomfort with the intimate details of Susan's dead body was becoming obvious.

"Look, you just hold tight to this file and keep working on whatever lead you think you've got. I need to regroup."

Niall understood and let me go.

≠

Mary and I had a lie-in the next morning until it was nearly noon. I could hear the hissing of the radiator as I laid in bed, nuzzling my face in Mary's soft breasts. The hissing gradually turned to clanking, and somewhere down the hall I could hear a man's voice cursing at it.

"Is that sodding thing starting up again?" Mary groaned. She stretched her arms out and nearly knocked a beer bottle off the bedside table.

I moaned into her chest, not wanting to get up. But the realization of self-employment reminded me that I had better start my day if I wanted to keep my apartment, broken radiator or not.

Mary joined me at Fresh Slab since it was Sunday, and we worked hard to clean the little place up and rearrange things so it wouldn't look so cluttered.

"Jon, did you move our clue box?"

"No, why?" I asked from behind a wall of cartons.

"It's not here."

I peered out at her. "What do you mean?"

She stood by the counter, empty-handed. "I mean, it's gone."

"Well, it's got to be here somewhere. Why would anyone take..." I stopped mid-thought. Had Mr. White snuck off with it the other day and I just didn't pay attention? Or what about Carol, who's been eyeing the stall lately? Who would have even known about it other than our readers?

As I was contemplating this, one of the boxes slipped out of my grip. It fell to the floor with a very solid thud.

"I hope those weren't 45's," Mary said, quickly changing the subject. She came over to help me and opened it to check.

"Jon, look at this."

The box was filled with ledger books and crumpled envelopes.

Mary pulled one of the books out and slowly began leafing through it. "Whoever did this bookkeeping was pretty sloppy." She pointed to a column. "This isn't even added correctly."

I dug through the box and took out a worn envelope addressed to Mr. White. It was a typed demand for payment with no return address and no indication of what it was for. The only clue to its tracking was the postmark from Crawley. I pulled another letter out and found the demand in that one more threatening.

"Do you think Mr. White was being blackmailed?" Mary asked after we had reviewed the questionable contents of the box.

It certainly looked that way to me. Could that have been the real reason for his rapid exodus from London?

"I bet Paul would like to see this," I said, pointing to the ledger book. "He used to pull his hair out trying to balance receipts with the account. Hell, we were just talking about how Mr. White never filled orders properly."

Mary's forehead wrinkled. "But this looks more like it was done on purpose. I mean, look closer."

She pointed out a section of the page that had heavy scribbling, like the writer was over-correcting a mistake. Except, when I deciphered the writing, I could see that the correct figure was underneath. It was, indeed, obvious that the numbers were being altered. I flipped further through the book and found more instances of the false reporting.

We closed the shop early and headed to Bugs' and Tony's place. If anyone knew about blackmailing, it was Tony and his 'friends' who lived in the flat above. No one spoke of it, but we all knew that's what paid their bills; Bugs' lousy Docklands job couldn't even cover a week's worth of shopping.

When we arrived at their flat, Bugs pulled us in anxiously.

"I've been trying to phone you all day, mate!" he exclaimed.

"What for?"

"I ran into Gangrene this morning," he replied. "Well, I mean, not exactly." He started to get a bit flustered. "I saw him in a phone box, so I snuck 'round behind some shrubbery and listened. He made a big deal for Wednesday. At the X-Ray Spex show."

My lips curled into a sly smile. "Good. Then we can nab his dealer and found out once and for all who it is. I'm betting on that answering a hell of a lot of questions."

Bugs nodded. "Same plan as last time?"

"Yeah, only this time we jump in as the deal goes down, not after. We can't let him get away again."

"Jonny boy," Tony said as he joined Bugs and me in the kitchen, "you don't need me to tell you this cunt is up to something."

Mary followed him in, carrying with her the ledger book that we wanted Tony to inspect.

"And I wouldn't be surprised if *he* was the one doing the blackmailing," Tony continued.

"But the letters were addressed *to* him," I protested.

Tony smirked and poked me in the forehead. "You need to think like a *criminal* to solve a crime, Jonny."

Mary's eyes sparkled at that, the way they did when she got a wild idea.

≠

I hadn't been at Fresh Slab for more than an hour the next morning when I heard a loud commotion in the Beaufort Market lobby. Boise Lou was outside Carol's stand throwing a complete fit. Carol and Brody were trying to calm him down, but it wasn't working. He punched his fists against the wall a couple times, fuming. Then he turned towards my stall.

Just great, I thought. *Now what?*

"You had better have the right answer for me, Hunter," Boise growled, yanking me by my collar to mere inches from his seething face. Brody rushed in behind him with Carol at his side.

"Lou, stop," Carol pleaded.

"What the fuck are you on about?" I spat at him, trying to squirm my way out of his grip.

"You *know* what I want, you bastard. If you don't tell me where Harlowe is right now I swear I'll snap your fucking neck." His eyes burned red.

Carol reached for his arm, but he shoved her back with his other hand, sending her to the floor.

"Boise, mate, come on now," Brody said fearfully as he went for Carol, whose eyes had begun to tear up.

I had to think fast.

Boise tightened his grip on me, making my t-shirt collar cut into my neck.

My hand reached behind me, and I felt for anything. The stapler registered against my fingers. I took it and cracked it against his skull as hard and as fast as I could. He instantly let go, falling back against Brody.

"Piss off, Boise!" I yelled at him. "It's not my job to keep track of your fucking tart!" I shoved my boot hard into him as he laid on the floor.

Brody dragged Boise out into the lobby, then helped him up.

"Your mate Coles is a dead man when I find him, Hunter," Boise rasped on his way out to King's Road.

I helped Carol up when the Teds had gone. She seemed unhurt aside from being a little shaken-up.

"Harlowe's gone missing," she said to me quietly. "No one's seen her in almost two days. And with all the craziness that's been going on lately..." Carol frowned.

I nodded as understandingly as I could muster at that moment. But my mind went to our clue: *it all started with Stacie.*

When I returned to the flat that evening, all was dark. I sighed at the prospect of having no electricity, but when I tried the switch, the lights went on just fine. Where was Mary? I knew she didn't start her extra hours yet, and she should have been home long before me.

I looked around the flat for her, but all I found was a note on the kitchen table:

> *Luv,*
> *I've got a lead I have to follow.*
> *Don't wait up for me.*
> *—Maire*

TWELVE

By morning, Mary still had not returned. Panic shivered through me. I scoured the flat looking for any clues to her whereabouts, but found nothing. She was gone, just like that, without a trace.

Frantically, I dialed numbers on the phone. Seamus McSurley said she hadn't shown up for work yet, Bugs and Tony assured me they hadn't seen her, Rachel and Michelle from Crawley didn't even know she was missing, and Nige's phone just rang and rang. I couldn't find Niall's number, but I determined that he'd be in classes at the university. And with our lack of cash, she wouldn't have been able to make it all the way over to Keely in Ireland.

Where could she have gone? And what lead was she following that was so urgent it couldn't have waited for me?

I took the next train to Sloane Square and rushed to Beaufort Market in case Mary had gone there. The keys to Fresh Slab were still in my pocket, but perhaps Carol had seen her come in. Any little thing would help me right now.

But Carol's stall wasn't open.

That's odd, I thought. *She's usually the first one here, and it's already almost noon.*

I looked for a little sign tacked up to remind her customers that she would be closed, but there was none. Just the plain metal gate hiding a darkened stall.

My next stop was McSurley's Pub. I prayed that I'd see Mary behind the counter pulling pints.

"Jon, lad," old McSurley called out as I entered. He was in Mary's place, tending the bar.

"Has Mary come in yet?" I asked nervously.

McSurley shook his head. "You two aren't in any trouble, I hope?" he asked, drying glasses.

I looked around the room for her, not wanting to make small talk.

"Because I've always told Maire Ailbhe if she needed anything to just ask," he continued. "I promised her mum I'd watch after her, rest her soul." McSurley stopped what he was doing for a moment to make the sign of the cross.

"When she comes in, just tell her I'm looking for her," I said to him, leaving without even a glance back.

Where else could she be?

St. Stephen's was close by, so I walked there thinking that perhaps Mary had gone to check on Paul. But Mary wasn't there either.

"Jon!" Paul rasped as I entered his room.

"Paul! You can see me!" My voice came out as an ecstatic shout. I ran to his side, my nervousness countered momentarily by the shock of seeing my best friend conscious again.

"I've got some brilliant scars, mate," he gloated. His face still needed some healing time, but much of the swelling had gone down, and I could tell that underneath the bruises he was beaming.

"You don't sound too good, though," I said, noting his raw voice.

He nodded his head as best he could. "They just took that fucking tube out of my throat, mate. But it'll be fine."

I had forgotten that he had machines breathing for him not that long ago.

"So, what happened?"

"There's not much to tell. I can't really remember anything after my date with Carol."

"You didn't see who did this to you?"

He shook his head gently. "I just remember feeling someone gripping my hand before the ambulance came. And yelling at me to keep breathing. A fucking crass bastard, he was."

I thought back to what the nurse had said to Mary and me the other night. "Jeffreys?"

"Yeah, that's him. The D. I. Who'd have thought, mate? A fucking *pig*." He laughed at the punk irony of it, then coughed a bit. "He's been in to see me a few times, too. Keeps asking if I saw the bloke, but I just can't remember."

"Have you seen Mary this morning?" I asked him, the feeling of worry starting to resurface now that I found Paul awake.

"No, mate." He stopped. "She's not..."

I shook my head. "No, no, she's fine. She left me a note to say she was checking something out and would be right back." I tried to hide my fear so that Paul wouldn't get excited. "I was just hoping to meet up with her a little early."

He relaxed a bit and leaned his head back into the pillow. "I bet Mr. White is pretty upset over my lack of attendance, eh?"

I smiled at Paul slightly. "Don't you worry about him. Everything's okay." I didn't feel I had time to give him the good news about his employment. Mary needed to be found and fast.

I said my goodbyes and waved down a bus. Unless Edwards had cut short his trip, it looked like Jeffreys was my only remaining option. I just hoped that Mary and Paul were right about his innocence.

Scotland Yard was not the romanticized place I had envisioned from my American childhood. It had been moved about seven years earlier to a new facility that took up a good block section and was relatively unadorned, with only windows as decorations.

When I entered, I was peaceably detained by security until they could locate Inspector Jeffreys. Nearly ten minutes passed before I saw him head into the lobby, by which time I could have really used a smoke. Mary must have taken the cigarettes out of my pocket.

"Well, well, what have we here?" Jeffreys asked snidely, removing the pen from his mouth to point at me. "You've got some information for me, I hope."

"I... I came here for your help, actually," I stammered.

Jeffreys chuckled loud enough that it caught the attention of a few other constables. "Oh, is that right? I thought I was just a pig?"

I sighed and looked away for a minute, feeling the blood rush to my face.

He eyed me once over, then motioned for me to follow him. We took the lift up a couple floors, then he led me to a glass booth in a back corner, apparently his office. Once at his desk, Jeffreys waited until I sat down in front of him before he took a seat himself.

"Your mate's come 'round, finally," he said, leaning back in his creaky chair.

I only nodded. The feeling of a panic attack was coming on, and my hands began to shake.

Jeffreys must have sensed this new tension because he pulled out a cigarette, lit it, and handed it to me. "So, what's with the sudden change of heart, then?"

I inhaled the smoke deeply before responding. My pulse was beating through my chest and there was nothing else I could do.

"My girlfriend is missing," I finally said to him.

Jeffreys sat up straight and looked at me seriously. "How long has she been gone?"

"An entire day."

"Well, that's not really..."

I took another hit of my cigarette and shook my head. "She left a note for me yesterday saying that she had a lead she had to follow, but that was it. She didn't say what it was or anything else. I've checked everywhere and phoned everyone, and no one has seen her or heard from her at all."

Jeffreys scribbled a few things down. "What do you think this lead might be?" he asked.

"I don't know. There were a few Teddy Boys we had our eyes on, so maybe she went to follow them. But I'm scared that she's in over her head. And I don't know what else to do."

Jeffreys put his pen to his teeth and bit down, staring at his notes. He did this in silence for quite some time, as though he had begun to ignore me.

"I might have something for you," I offered after a couple minutes, hoping it would elicit his help since my groveling didn't seem to do it. "Dan Green has a deal going down tomorrow night with this new dealer he's been using."

That did it. Jeffreys looked up at me, then his lips pursed pensively.

I continued: "If you and Edwards are there, maybe between all of us we can finally nab him and see who this new guy is."

Jeffreys smiled and leaned back in his chair again, pointing his newly-gnawed pen at me. "Yeah, I'll help you."

I headed to King's College when I left Scotland Yard, hoping to find Mary working with Niall on his research. Niall was in the lab, but Mary hadn't been there at all.

"Any news on the pathologist?" I asked, trying to hide my disappointment.

Niall sighed as he gathered Susan's paperwork together. "Mervyn. His name is Mervyn. And he's charming." He flipped through the pages, tidying and re-organizing them. "Pleased that I was doing well in my studies. Very encouraging. Got on brilliantly with the coroner's officers. Just lovely."

"Wait. What are you saying?"

Niall stopped and looked at me with angry eyes.

"I'm saying that we'll find nothing on him there. I don't know who the hell this bloke is, but he's got the coroner's office wrapped around his bloody finger."

I didn't understand. "But, if you've been going there all this time now and never heard of him, how can he be so connected?"

"I just don't know." Niall rubbed his eyes. "Even Poirot didn't have it this bleeding tough."

I frowned with him.

"I'm sorry," Niall continued. "I'm sorry I made you risk so much for... so little."

"No." I gripped his shoulder. "This isn't the end. Somehow, this is important. It has to be."

Niall looked down at his shoes.

"You... just protect this." I handed Susan's file to him.

He held the file tightly and nodded. "I promise."

I promise. That was it. The voice at the coroner's office. The one I recognized. The proverbial light bulb clicked on inside me. Standing there, it all fell into place. The pieces of the puzzle locked themselves together to form a terrifying, but complete, picture.

I rushed back to my flat, bursting in with the hope of finding Mary there. But the only thing I found was the darkness that had been there when I left that morning. Nothing had been moved, and there was still no trace of Mary. I called around to my mates again, but the answers remained unchanged. Wherever she was, I prayed she was holding her own, at least until I could find her.

My nerves were shot, and so I tried to numb myself with a couple cans of lager. I was scared for Mary, but I was also scared for what would transpire the following evening. If my deduction was correct, I was going to need Scotland Yard's help. And I was going to need that gun I hid at Fresh Slab.

I rang Bugs back and asked him to have

Tony get hold of some bullets that would fit it. From what I could hear on the other end, Tony was more than willing to oblige.

"Meet me at Beaufort Market tomorrow before the show, mate," I said to him.

"Who do you think it is?" Bugs asked.

I hesitated for a moment. "I... I don't want to say just yet. But I'm going to need some back-up."

Bugs chuckled softly on the other end. "Oh, we'll be there, all right. We'll be there with *friends*."

Tony said something, but I couldn't hear what it was. Bugs laughed snidely at Tony's comment. By '*friends*,' I assumed he meant the thugs who lived upstairs from him, and this time that was fine by me.

I thought through a plan until I eventually fell asleep from exhaustion.

A ringing telephone woke me up in the morning. It was Jeffreys.

"Nothing yet on your girlfriend," he said. "Have you heard from her at all?"

"No, not a word."

Jeffreys sighed. "I'll issue a full search and see what we come up with. I've got panda cars in the area."

I shivered, anticipating the worst.

"We'll find her," he replied to my nervous silence. "No one else is dying on *my* watch."

That didn't really make me feel better, but it would have to do.

"You better bring some constables with you tonight. I have a feeling it's not going to be pretty... and you're not going to like it."

"What the hell do you mean by that?" he coughed out, clearing his throat.

"Just meet me at Beaufort Market before the show, and try to blend in."

I heard him sigh. "Bloody punks," he grumbled as we hung up.

Tonight's the night, I told myself. I rubbed my hands together and got ready.

The show was being held at The Man in the Moon, a pub located between Beaufort Market and Seditionaries. The lead singer of the main band playing, Poly Styrene, ran a stall next to Fresh Slab, so I knew the show was going to draw a local crowd. Which meant all the suspects would be there.

It took a while for me to retrieve the gun since I shoved it into the shelf space pretty deeply, but eventually I found it. To keep it out of sight, I hid it in my jacket pocket.

Bugs and Tony arrived on schedule, joined by three menacing blokes.

"This here's Gusty, Vinny, and Lon." Tony pointed to each as he introduced them.

I nodded in greeting. They said nothing.

"So, we're gonna teach Nige a lesson tonight, eh, Jonny Boy?" Tony said, nudging me excitedly.

"We just might," I replied.

"You got the gun?" Bugs asked, picking his teeth with his fingernail.

I pulled it out of my pocket. "You got the bullets?"

Tony placed a small box on the counter.

"You don't even know how to use that thing, you poof," Bugs snapped, snatching the gun away from me. He tore open the box and filled the barrel with bullets.

"Nah, Bugs, Jonny here is starting to get himself some bollocks," Tony said proudly, patting me on the back. "He's finally doing things *Tony's* way."

"Now watch me, alright?" Bugs said to me. "You aim it like this, lock the hammer, and brace yourself when you pull the trigger because the force is stronger than you think." He held the gun out securely and looked as though he was intent on shooting something. "See?"

"Yeah, I got it."

Bugs smirked at me and dropped the gun back in my hands. "We'll see about that," he said snidely.

"Hey, now, leave the bloke alone," Tony replied in my defense. "He'll be just fine."

Bugs rolled his eyes.

Tony leaned in to me. "Just watch that we're out of the way, alright mate?" he whispered, patting me on the back again.

"Remember to aim for his chest or stomach. Some place nice and painful. Or his face. That'll get him," Bugs said, grinning with anticipation.

"I don't want to *kill* him," I replied. "I want him to rot in prison so he can..."

Bugs groaned. "I can't *believe* this!"

Tony shook his head. "Here you go again, Jonny. You need to stop trying to make the world a better place and start thinking of Suz and Jules. Of your mate Paul."

"And *Mary*," Bugs interjected. He always knew right where to stick the knife in.

I opened my mouth to protest, but it would have to wait.

THIRTEEN

"Oh...just what we need," Bugs said loudly. "A fucking *pig*."

In walked Jeffreys, as promised.

"You better watch your mouth, you little ponce," Jeffreys spat at him.

"And what are you gonna do in your wee punk outfit?"

"Bugs, shut the fuck up already," I scolded nervously. "He's on *our* side."

Bugs cackled.

"I'm serious! I asked him to help us, and I don't need you drawing attention to him. We need everyone to think he's one of us."

"*Me* draw attention to *him*? Ha!"

Jeffreys pointed a chewed pen at Bugs. "Don't try me. I'll have you back at the station quicker than you think."

I looked Jeffreys over and had to laugh a little to myself. He had dressed in plainclothes, alright, but his attempt at being 'punk' was not too successful. It looked like he had cut perfectly-aligned holes in his Rolling Stones t-shirt, stuck a few random safety pins in the material, and put on a pair of slept-in jeans. The jeans might be able to pass, but the shirt? And his clean-cut hair?

"No one's gonna buy that," Tony blurted out, having inspected Jeffreys as well.

"He's right, Jeffreys. You look like a fucking hippie."

Bugs laughed at him, going back to picking his teeth.

"Well," Jeffreys growled, "*make* it work!" His face was reddening a little.

I stared at him for a minute, then reached behind the counter for a black marker. "First things first."

He watched as I wrote "*I hate*" above the Rolling Stones' name on his shirt. Then I stretched some of the cuts into genuine rips and safety-pinned the larger ones.

"You really think that'll do it?" he asked me.

Bugs' laugh had turned to a snicker.

Before Jeffreys could protest, I brought my hands to his head and messed his hair til most of it stood up.

"Hey!"

"*Now* we can go," I replied, pleased with the transformation.

Jeffreys grumbled, but the scowl on his face only helped to assimilate him into the crowd. I was confident no one would recognize him. As long as Bugs stayed away from us, that is.

"You, Tony, and the gang go mingle with everyone. When it's half past eleven and Gangrene gets ready to make his deal, meet us near the back where he said he'd be," I told Bugs. "Jeffreys and I will jump the guy, but we might need your help if he makes a run for it."

"And someone grab Green while you're at it," Jeffreys added. "I want that bastard off the streets."

As we were about to split up, a familiar voice drifted over the growing crowd.

"*Jon!*" Mary yelled from across the room.

My pulse quickened anxiously as she and Keely meandered their way through people to get to me.

"Maire! Where the bloody hell have you been?" I asked, grabbing her and clutching her to my chest possessively. I squeezed her tight enough it elicited a squeak. Keely leaned in and I held her close for a moment as well. I don't think I had ever felt happier to see those two crazy girls.

"I was following Nige. You wouldn't believe what we found."

"Yeah, well, don't worry; Jeffreys and I are nabbing the bloke tonight."

Mary glanced over at Jeffreys who was standing beside me.

"Boy, do *you* look different," she said to him, giggling under her breath.

Jeffreys smirked. "Edwards and I sent half the squad out to look for you," he replied.

"Well, I almost needed it, too. Jon, I don't know what Nige is up to, but it's no good. He ran off with Harlowe yesterday and we followed them to the train station."

"I heard him buy tickets to what sounded like the Cotswolds," added Caoilinn. She pursed her lips and made a 'surprised' face, like she had just given me the final clue to solve the mystery.

"What the fuck would they be going there for? Holiday?"

Mary shrugged. "I don't know. All I know is that they didn't board the train. Some bloke showed up, then one of the trains arrived and we lost sight of them. When the crowd left, they were gone. We haven't been able to locate them since."

Jeffreys chewed on his pen. "Nige," he said, thinking aloud.

"Nigel Coles," Mary offered.

"Nigel *Coles*," he repeated, apparently searching his memory for something. He sucked on the pen until it was too mangled to do anything else with it, then tossed it to the floor and pulled a new one out of his jeans pocket. "Nope, nothing. Never heard of him."

"Well, of course you haven't," I quipped. "He's never done anything!"

"Then why the hell are you bothering with him?"

I sighed. "Because most of the girls who've died so far were girlfriends of his."

"Is he a junkie?" Jeffreys asked.

I shook my head.

"Forget about him. It's probably a coincidence. Or someone trying to frame him."

"How can you just..."

"I've been a detective a little longer than you, son," Jeffreys interrupted me. "I should think I know what I'm doing." He took a fresh chomp on his pen.

"Hey, there goes Gangrene," Mary said, pointing at the sorry sod's grizzled form. "Are we still watching out for him?"

"Yeah. Bugs caught him setting up a deal for tonight, and we're going to get them."

Keely rested her manicured hand on my shoulder. "Do you think this is the last of it?" she asked. Mary had filled her in on the whole sordid tale.

"I sure hope so," I replied, glancing back at her. I could smell the sweet scent of shampoo in her long auburn hair. Mary kissed her once on the lips softly, then moved to my other side and did the same to me.

"Come on," Jeffreys said, frowning. "It's nearly eleven. Let's get in position."

We all looked at each other, then Keely pulled her hair up and back, pinning it atop her head. She gave me a wink, and I knew I was ready, come what may.

$$\neq$$

The X-Ray Spex were playing down in the basement of the pub, as they usually did on Wednesday nights. It was cave-like, dark and claustrophobic with a low ceiling. The crowd had dispersed early on when the opening band, The Ants, started playing, perhaps thinking them daft. But Mary and I thought they were brilliant, and we recognized the singer as Stuart, one of the blokes who hung around Seditionaries. Once the Ants had left the stage, though, much of the crowd returned. It was really just us King's Road regulars, so only about a hundred people, but within that space it was more than enough to keep our mission secret.

Poly was wailing away at the microphone, song after song, and Jeffreys cringed through most of it. Thankfully, Bugs stayed away from him while he was complaining, otherwise he might have blown Jeffreys' cover.

When we split up, the girls and I stuck together on one side of the room while Jeffreys said he'd cover the other. I accounted for Bugs' and Tony's gang near the bar that ran the length of one wall, and we waved to each other that we were ready. But when I turned back, Jeffreys was gone.

"That bastard! I thought he said he'd help us!"

Mary looked around. "Maybe he's just trying to get in closer or something?"

I searched for him again among the punks, but still couldn't find him. There weren't many places to hide, so where could he have gone other than out?

"Damn it!" I cursed.

"Never mind him, then," Mary said quickly. "This is all about us, anyway. So, let's just get the job done."

I sighed for a moment, then gathered myself together. "Right. You and Keely take Gangrene until Tony and the guys get to him, and I'll jump the dealer."

"It's a plan," the girls replied in agreement.

We looked at each other. Mary squeezed my hand tightly for a moment before giving me a smile. Keely pressed a finger to her lips then put it to my nose.

Gangrene checked his watch and hobbled to the back of the room. The three of us moved stealthily towards him in the shadows. He leaned on his crutches after a minute or two, looking around impatiently.

I could feel my own heart racing. Mary touched my shoulder reassuringly, shivering, herself. We were so close, I couldn't have a heart attack and screw it up now.

Five minutes passed and still nothing. Gangrene hobbled back and forth a bit until finally someone approached.

A tall, dark man reached his hand into his trench coat and pulled out a wrapped bundle. Gangrene took it and slipped over a wad of cash to him.

"It's now or never," I whispered to Mary, and we pounced.

She knocked Gangrene over in one fell swoop. He grabbed at her hair, but she punched him right in the face.

Keely wasn't so violent, but she was bigger and stronger than Mary. She held Gangrene down as best as she could, writhing atop him as she fought his flailing arms. It was a good thing she had on trousers instead of her usual dresses, or there would have been quite a delicious show. As it was, I already couldn't help feeling excited by the crazy energy with which Mary and Keely were doing their job.

Seeing the scuffle, the mystery man started to make a run for it. I reached for his coat but only got air as he opened a security door out to the back alley. Stumbling forward, I followed him outside. He tried to out-run me but tripped on something in the dark, buying me enough time to catch up with him.

His fists struck at me as I approached, and he wrestled me down to the ground. I could feel glass cutting into my waist where my shirt had crept up. He knocked my head into the ground once, but I rolled out of the way of a second blow. His hand reached for me again, but I was quick enough to yank it. I pulled him down to my level and tried to head-butt him. He dodged it and countered with a backhand to my nose. I felt a crunch and then the warmth of blood trickling down over my top lip. We were like feral cats now, panting and growling and clawing at each other for dominance. I gave him every bit of energy I had, but he continued to have the upper hand.

After another heated round, he finally moved to stand up. I grabbed at his trousers, holding him still for a moment. Grunting, he pulled me up where I could see his face. The patch over his eye was visible in the moonlight and his silver hair gave away the secret he had been hiding all this time. I reached for his throat, but he let loose a mad punch to my stomach.

"You fucking cunt! I *knew* it!" I whimpered, falling to my knees in pain. "You'll never get away with this!"

Edwards laughed heartily as he grabbed my hair and cracked my face into his knee. "I've been getting away with this for months now!" He kicked me in the groin, shoving me back to the ground in a heap.

"I'll tell them all," I rasped, coughing up blood.

"And who's going to believe *you*, Mr. Hunter?" He leaned forward, ready to continue his assault.

"*I* will." Jeffreys' voice echoed through the alleyway.

Edwards' eye widened for a moment. Then, growling in betrayal, he lunged at Jeffreys.

"You bleeding amateur," Edwards hissed. His fist landed as a thud against Jeffreys' chest.

"You had Green in your grasp time and time again."

—*Another punch*—

"And you let him go..."

Jeffreys swung back, missing.

"You let him go and another man's daughter died."

I tried to drag myself nearer to them, feeling more broken than I ever have.

Edwards' knuckles cracked against Jeffreys' face. "And then another man's daughter." He punched again. "And another..."

"Enough!" I yelled, stabbing a hunk of broken pint glass from the ground into Edwards' shoe.

He merely kicked at my head, the glass apparently not sharp enough to cut through the leather.

But I bought Jeffreys enough time to recover so he could land a few punches himself.

"Oh, you may think you're above the law, Mervyn," Jeffreys spat, "but you're not above the law of the *streets*." He shoved Edwards back against a skip. The Chief Inspector's body made a hollow thud against the metal receptacle. "Go ahead, think I'm a fucking amateur. I got a lot less to lose than you."

Edwards gasped for air and whipped out something shiny. "Actually..."

God no! My hands were sticky with blood, but I had to try. I ground my teeth to absorb the pain while I forced myself to my knees. Quickly, I scrambled to get the gun out of my pocket.

Trying to remember what Bugs told me, I cocked the hammer, aimed at the tallest figure, and fired.

The blast knocked me back violently.

I heard a yelp, and a body crumpled down to the ground, holding his leg. The other bloke made a desperate dash towards me.

"Where the hell did you get that?" Jeffreys panted as he leaned in to help me up.

Relieved to see that I hit the right guy, I reached for his hand. "I took it away from Green."

"I could toss you in jail for what you just did, you know."

I let out a breathless chuckle.

Jeffreys' waiting constables ran into the alley from the street, having heard the shot. Most of them crowded around Edwards, who was still on the ground moaning.

"Take *him* away, first," Jeffreys said to the policemen, pointing over at Edwards.

The door from the pub opened and the girls rushed out to find me.

"Jon!" Mary cried frantically, her hands reaching for me to assess the damage.

"It's over now, Maire," I said to her softly.

Jeffreys shook his head angrily. "I can't fucking believe this. How did you know?"

Keely wrapped her arms around me carefully and let me rest my weight on her.

"The marble in our tin of clues," I coughed, wincing as the girls tried to keep me standing upright.

He looked at me quizzically, passing my response off as delirium from the nice beating I'd just gotten. "Look, I'll have a panda car take you home. Go and get some rest. I'll talk to you tomorrow."

Mary, Keely, and I agreed wordlessly and slowly headed out through the alley. As we passed, I could hear a constable say to Jeffreys: "That's a new look for you, Inspector." Jeffreys' crass voice replied: "Yeah? Well, piss off!"

Jeffreys was at my flat the next morning, bright and early.

"Don't you have a lift around here that works?" he panted.

"Be happy the electricity hasn't cut out yet," I retorted from the couch, trying to put things in perspective. Niall was leaning over me, tending to my wounds.

Jeffreys huffed and closed the apartment door behind him.

"How about some tea, then?" Mary offered from the kitchen. She wasn't exactly dressed for company, clad only in a black bra and a pair of my boxers, but then modesty was never one of her virtues. Behind her, Keely was plating hot scones.

Mary brought us out cups of tea, then took a seat next to me on the couch. Keely followed, sharing the product of her culinary talent with us before sitting cross-legged on the floor near Niall.

"So, now, how is it again that you figured out Edwards was the culprit?" Jeffreys asked, taking a big gulp of tea and burning his tongue.

"Well, it's not so easy as that."

"Yeah? I've got time. Looks like you do, too," he said, eyeing my condition in the light.

I sighed.

Mary got up and rummaged through a kitchen cabinet, pulling out the old tin we kept the clues in. She dumped the contents on a plate and handed it to Jeffreys.

"Hey, this is Edwards' *eye*," Jeffreys exclaimed, holding up the item we previously thought was a marble.

"I didn't figure that out until..."

"We just thought it was trash from the alley," Mary interrupted.

"How did it end up here?"

"My mate Bugs and I were following Green at the Clash show...er, riot. We saw he was making a deal, so Bugs went out back to nab the dealer. He didn't get him, obviously, but they got into a scuffle. After punching the bloke in the face, Bugs said he heard a tooth fall to the ground. But when he searched around for it, all he found was that."

I pointed to the glass eye.

"We had no idea it was his eye that was knocked out," I explained.

"And this whole time lately I thought it was Nige," Mary sighed.

"I did too," I replied, placing my hand on her knee. "Especially after I found him at Sloane

Square with a nice black eye the day after the show."

Niall fidgeted nervously during our conversation, then finally pulled out Susan's file from the cushion behind him. He handed it to Jeffreys.

"Where on earth did you get this?" Jeffreys asked, putting down his tea.

I could see fear in Niall's eyes as he began to confess: "I…"

"I nicked it," I interjected. "From Edwards."

Jeffreys gave me a look of incredulity.

Niall continued: "I wanted to find out about the pathologist. Because it was the same bloke for all the murders. M. U."

"Only, we read it wrong," I added. "The signature was M. E. E."

"Mervyn Edwards," Jeffreys answered.

"My aunt told me that he had served as a medic in the war, so I knew he must have had some credentials."

"So, what about the Stacie thing?" Keely asked. This was all news to her and Mary since they had been out tracking Nige instead.

"Stacie was Edwards' daughter," I answered. "And Gangrene was her dealer. I figured that out when my aunt kept on about how sick she was before she died."

Jeffreys nodded. "We had a fine time interrogating Edwards and your grotty mate. Had us believing all this time that she died from an allergic reaction. Never thought that little thing was a junkie." He frowned.

Mary's eyes began to tear up. "So, are you saying that Susan had to die because the Chief Inspector wanted revenge?"

I ran my hand over her hair.

Jeffreys shrugged gently. "It looks that way, I'm afraid. Unless he can tell us something else."

Mary wiped at her eyes with the back of her hand silently.

"It really was the perfect crime for him," I said somberly. "If he hadn't made the mistake of getting Suz, no one would have ever known it was murder. And if we hadn't called him on it, he probably wouldn't have attacked Paul."

"He knew you were on his trail," Keely said, understanding.

"Well, I've got a proposition," Jeffreys announced, finishing off his cup of tea. "We could use an informant like you."

I wrinkled my face. "You've got to be off your rocker."

Work for the pigs? Wouldn't that be throwing my ethics out the window?

"So, you're all talk then?" he remarked snidely.

"What's that supposed to mean?"

"You gonna live your life by song lyrics? Or are you gonna be that change you shout about?"

"How is being a snitch going to do anything but cost me friends?"

Jeffreys laughed. "I don't need a snitch. I need a partner."

I looked away at Keely. She raised her eyebrows for a moment, but didn't say anything.

"You want to change things in the world? You gotta be *inside* the system to rough it up. Why do you think I'm there?"

Mary patted the bandages around my waist in agreement and I looked back at him.

He was right.

Jeffreys smiled. "Good." He stood up, collecting himself and dumping the plate of clues into his pocket.

"I was looking for these," he said, noting the chewed pens we found, apparently a false lead set at the scene by Edwards.

Mary curled herself up against me and we watched him from our warm spot on the couch.

"I'll be in touch." Jeffreys pointed at me with a new pen. "Oh, and here's a little something from the Loss Adjuster."

He placed a wad of pound notes on the chair, then gave an upward nod, closing the door behind him.

Mary tilted her head up to kiss me, and I couldn't help but laugh aloud.

Jon Hunter, newest 'snout' of the C.I.D.!